WARRIOR'S PRIDE

Toyah Chama rode at the front of the line, to be first to see movement on the dark prairie in front of them. Suddenly, his pony gave a warning snort and halted, flaring its nostrils to catch a scent from somewhere ahead. Then Chama saw the outlines of more than a dozen horsemen, moving across the moonlit hills.

"*To-ho-baka,*" he whispered, the Comanche word for an enemy, warning the others to stay silent.

Slowly the riders moved south, until Chama heard a distant cry in the white man's tongue.

"There they are . . . I see them!"

Suddenly the horsemen turned and charged, the sound of spurs rattling against their horses' sides, as hooves beat along the dry prairie.

Chama brought his Spencer to his shoulder, trying to find a target among the *Tosi Tivo*. He picked a rider at the front of the pack and fired. The sound of the gun was a good sound. It was better to fight and die, than to wait in the stink of Fort Sill for death to creep up on him while he slept.

It was better to die like a warrior.

THE LAST WARRIOR

FREDERIC BEAN

ZEBRA BOOKS
KENSINGTON PUBLISHING CORP.

ZEBRA BOOKS

are published by

Kensington Publishing Corp.
475 Park Avenue South
New York, NY 10016

Copyright © 1992 by Frederic Bean

First printing: June, 1992

Printed in the United States of America

1

A solitary Indian sat on a high, windswept bluff beneath a live oak tree, watching the sun lower in the western sky. Twin braids of coarse gray hair hung below the old man's shoulders as Toyah Chama sat cross-legged, dreaming of his past. Below the bluff the parched ground returned the fierce rays of the sun with shimmering mirages, like water in the distance. But there was no water. Rain had not fallen at the Fort Sill Reservation all summer, and as fall drew near, the ground cracked open, surrendering the last drops of deep moisture in the bowels of the earth. In the white man's year 1908, a terrible drought had come to southwestern Oklahoma, burning the land to a cinder. But the old warrior was not looking at the dry land, or thinking of the starving sheep and cattle on the grassless prairie beyond the bluff, for he was lost in dreams of a distant past, when his people roamed free on the Staked Plains. In his dream, Chama was a young warrior again, swinging under the neck of his fast-charging pony with a rifle against his shoulder, firing at the enemy with deadly skill, racing through the galloping blue-coat soldiers without fear of their bullets. The air was filled with the war whoops of his warriors, and the screams of frightened horses and wounded soldiers. Again and again he fired his rifle, killing so many of the enemy he lost count. Painted warriors and swirling ponies were all around him, sending a choking cloud of dust into the air. It was a wonderful dream, filled with good memories of the days when the Kwahadie Comanches feared no enemy on mother earth, defeating the *Tosi Tivo* soldiers in battle, then riding swiftly to the safety of the endless canyons of the Palo Duro, to celebrate their victory and kill more of the plentiful buffalo.

Slowly the dream faded, replaced by sad memories of the last days of freedom on the plains, when Mackenzie came with two thousand blue-coats to surround Chief Buffalo Hump in the canyon. In equal number the *Tosi Tivo* soldiers were no match for mounted Comanches, but when Mackenzie came, there were so many they blotted out the sun. Chief Buffalo Hump could send only a hundred and seventy warriors to protect the trail leading to the village. Chama and the others fought bravely, until all their bullets and arrows were gone, defeated for the first time in the history of The People.

Chama remembered, thinking of the eighteen "taums" of imprisonment at Fort Sill, since the battle in Palo Duro canyon. For eighteen taums, the Comanches, what was left of the Penatekas, the Noconas, and the Kwahadies, had been prisoners on the bleak reservation, crowded together with their old enemies the Kiowas. Starving, broken in spirit, and sick from the white man's diseases, the last of the great Comanche nation were nothing more than sheep, waiting for a handout of moldy flour and rancid beef from the Indian Agent. For eighteen taums, Chama watched his people die, all the brave warriors who fought alongside him against the *Tosi Tivo* enemy, now only gaunt skeletons with sad eyes. The Great Spirit Powva had turned His back on His people, allowing them to perish at the hands of the *Tosi Tivo* in such a way, for it was not the brave death of a warrior, dying slowly of starvation and sickness.

From the beginning, Chama begged some of the old ones to follow him in an escape from the reservation. Many times, he talked with Buffalo Hump and Santana, pleading for a breakout from the misery of Fort Sill. But the word of War Chief Quannah was given in the treaty . . . the Comanches would never fight the *Tosi Tivo* again. Powva would send no sign to guide the Comanches from the reservation, even when Chama fasted the required four days, chewing peyote buttons and praying day and night with the ancient prayers. No sign came, only empty skies and silence.

Thus, in the summer of his seventy-first taum, Toyah Chama decided his time had come. He could endure the reservation no longer. At seventy-one, Powva could call him to begin the spirit journey very soon. Chama would not begin the walk toward death with the stink of Fort Sill in his nose. In two days, with the first full moon, he would pick two good ponies and escape, even if none of the others would follow him, even if Powva gave him no sign. It was better to die making his escape—caught by the *Tosi Tivo* soldiers

7

before he reached the Palo Duro—than to wait for slow death among the Kiowas. One last Comanche warrior would ride free across the plains, to spend his last days on mother earth as a free man. If death came at the hands of the soldiers, it was a better way to die than waiting at the fort for death to come for him while he slept.

Chama saw a dust cloud on the horizon, and knew at once that the old marshal was coming for him. Among the white men he had known, Marshal Sam Ault was the only one who seemed to understand the heart of a Comanche. Man-Who-Wears-The-Star had seen almost as many taums as Chama, better than sixty, and was the man Agent Tatum sent to bring Chama back to the fort each time he came to the bluff. Unlike other white men, Sam Ault would listen to the sorrow in Chama's heart, before he drove him back to the fort in the noisy carriage-with-no-horse. Chama hated the wagon Sam drove, smelling foul and making a great noise that startled the ponies. The marshal was a fine horseman. Chama could not understand why he had given up his horses to drive such a thing.

Chama watched the dust cloud, listening to the angry sound that broke the quiet around the bluff. Chama knew he could not let Sam Ault look into his eyes, for the wise old marshal might see his spirit, and know his plan to escape the reservation. It was time to pray for the spirit shield, to keep Sam from seeing the truth in Chama's eyes.

The wagon bounced over the dry ground and jolted to a stop, hissing smoke from its nose like a pony's breath on a cold morning. Sam got out and walked stiffly toward the live oak tree where Chama sat, a grin spread over his sun-blackened face. He no longer wore his gun, as he had during the first years when the Comanches came to Fort Sill. He no longer needed a gun, for there was no one left to fight. The Comanches stopped fighting eighteen taums ago, and were now nothing more than sheep.

"You know why I have come," Sam said, speaking Comanche as he took a seat on the ground in front of Chama. "It is the law. You cannot come out here without permission from Tatum."

Chama answered rapidly in Comanche, unable to hide his anger.

"A Comanche ear does not hear white man's law."

Sam grinned again, a twinkle in his deep blue eyes. A drooping hatbrim covered his face in shadow, but it did not hide the humor on his leathery face. Even for a *Tosi Tivo* he was tall, over six feet, with high cheekbones. Sam spoke the Comanche tongue fluently, with no accent, serving as interpreter for Agent Tatum at Fort Sill.

"I have no choice," Sam replied, this time in English. "We have been through this before. Tatum tells me you've been missing two or three days. It's time to go back."

"Forked Tongue Tatum does not own me. I am not one of his ponies."

"I'm only doin' my job, Chama. It's the law."

Chama's face was expressionless as Sam studied the wrinkled lines and braids of silver hair. Sam tried to remember how old Chama would be, thinking back to the day Mackenzie brought the last of the warlike Kwahadies to Fort Sill, the last Comanche band to stop fighting. Mackenzie's troops had forced the two hundred or so Comanches to walk the four-hundred-mile trek from Texas to Oklahoma in leg irons. By any standard it was extreme cruelty, yet hardly any worse than slaughtering the unarmed women and children in the Kwahadie village during the battle at Palo Duro. Mackenzie and Crook hated the Comanches above all other Indians, blaming them for more lost troopers' lives than any other tribe. Particularly the Antelope Band, the Kwahadies. No one would argue that the Comanches were the worst of the lot, the most skillful fighters, well known for the torture and mutilation of enemies. The Comanches were easily the most skilled horsemen Sam had ever seen, and certainly the best fighters. Years before, the Comanches whipped the Apaches and Cheyennes, then the Kiowas and Arapahos, until there was no one left to challenge them. For many years, the Kwahadies outfought the cavalry of Miles, Crook, and Mackenzie, until so many troopers were put afield, they outnumbered the Kwahadies ten to one. Finally, surrounded by two thousand bluecoats, Chief Buffalo Hump surrendered at Palo Duro. They had eaten the last of their camp dogs and ponies, they were out of ammunition, and dying of starvation with no place to run. Among them was Toyah Chama, Voice of the Wild Boar, War Chief of the Sata Exiponi, the elite Comanche warrior society. Even back then, maybe twenty years ago, Chama was considered old for a warrior, yet he killed so many soldiers at Palo Duro, that Mackenzie ordered him shot. Only orders from General Crook spared his life, as the last of the Comanches were driven on foot to Fort Sill, to prove to the other tribes that the last Comanches surrendered to live in peace on the reservation. Crook wanted a great fighter like Chama among the prisoners, as an example to the others.

Sam remembered, as he gazed at the frail old man sitting under the live oak. All of the Comanches settled into reservation life, finished with the war against the soldiers, leaving the old ways behind. All but one. Toyah Chama would never be a tame Indian. The ferocity was still buried in his eyes, and in his soul. Like some wild horses, his spirit could never be broken, not even after eighteen years of prison at Fort Sill.

Perhaps for this reason, Sam had taken a liking to Chama. He enjoyed their talks about the old days, for like Sam, Chama was nearing the end of his road through life. It was good, sometimes, to remember the way things used to be.

"You're up to somethin', ain't you?" Sam asked, searching Chama's face. "This is the second time in six months you've walked up here. I asked around this morning at the fort, just to see if you're still tryin' to talk some of the others into leaving the reservation again. I figured, after all this time, you'd give up on such a crazy notion. Hell, you're an old man now, Chama. Like me. Can't neither one of us ride a horse all day, like we used to. Somethin' tells me you're at it again, thinkin' about running off some place."

Chama would not look into Sam's eyes, fearing the white man might see his plan to escape.

"I am ready to die. I came here to sing my death song. *Suvate* . . . that is all."

Chama tried desperately not to think about his weapons, the old Spencer carbine and the bow and arrows buried in a deerskin under his shack at the fort. He prayed for the spirit shield to come in front of his eyes, so that Sam Ault would not see his plan to run away to the Palo Duro with the first full moon.

"I don't believe you," Sam replied. "I think you've come up here for good medicine on your journey."

Chama did not reply, gazing off at the setting sun.

Sam got up painfully, rubbing his arthritic knees, and went to the Star touring car for a pint of whiskey. He pulled the bottle from a pouch under the seat and walked back to the shade of the tree.

"Here," Sam said, offering Chama the bottle. "Have a drink of *Boisah Pah*. Then we'll start back."

Chama shook his head. Sam wanted him to drink the crazy water so the spirit shield would leave his eyes, telling Sam what he wanted to know about Chama's plans.

"No. *Boisah Pah* is for *Tosi Tivo*. You drink it."

Sam shrugged, then took a pull from the bottle.

"But you'll chew those damn peyote buttons all day long, which makes you crazy as a sack of loons. This is safer."

Chama stared blankly at the horizon, wishing for an end to this talk. He prayed for the spirit shield, and would not look into the clear blue eyes of the marshal.

"Let's go," Sam sighed, coming to his feet. "Gettin' late."

Chama got up slowly, shouldering his waterskin as he cast a final look at the setting sun. Suddenly, he saw something that brought his eyes into sharp focus. Overhead, a bird circled lazily in the air. Chama felt his heart beat faster. It was Quinne, the eagle, the most powerful spirit sign of all. There had been no eagles near Fort Sill in his memory, and now, a white-tailed Quinne flew above his head. It was a message no

Comanche could ignore. A powerful spirit sign.

As Chama watched, the great bird turned and flew west as hard as it could flap its wings, soon just a distant speck against the sunset. Quinne had flown as straight as an arrow toward the Palo Duro, even though the Chama homeland was four hundred miles away. A message, sent to the spirit of a Comanche. Follow the eagle. The spirit meaning was clear. Chama had been given his sign. Powva had answered his prayers at last.

Sam gave Chama a knowing look.

"Is that what you've been waitin' for, you old fox? Does that eagle mean big medicine?"

Chama quickly hid his eyes from the marshal. But Sam was not looking at Chama, the marshal was watching the speck disappear against the setting sun.

"Hadn't seen an eagle in these parts in a long time," Sam said thoughtfully. "I suppose this drought has pushed 'em off their range to find food."

Chama turned for the wagon-with-no-horse, suddenly dizzy with the excitement of his medicine sign. He almost fell to his knees, until Sam caught his arm to steady him.

"Been too long without food, Chama. An old man like you has gotta eat pretty regular. Hell, you ain't big around as a wet rope to begin with. You're gonna starve to death. Time you faced the fact that you ain't a young buck anymore, old friend. Like me, your time is 'bout used up."

Chama shook off Sam's hand and climbed in the seat.

"It is true, *Tosi Tivo*. I am old and useless."

Sam chuckled and shrugged his big shoulders.

"Same as me. The world is changin' mighty fast, and I ain't sure I belong anymore. Like this damn contraption I'm ridin' in, it don't suit me. I don't even understand how it works, but I've gotten too damn old to ride a horse all day. My joints won't let me ride anymore."

Chama understood most of the white man's words, yet he said nothing, gazing off at the horizon, keeping his eyes from the marshal. In the years Chama had spent at Fort Sill, he learned some English, more than he would admit to Agent Tatum. Chama spoke the *Tosi Tivo* words only when he had no choice.

Sam set the spark and walked to the front of the car. After two failed attempts, he cranked the motor to life, sputtering and belching smoke as the frame shook with the irregular beat of the engine.

Sam climbed in his seat, again noticing that Chama would not look at him for even a moment.

"Ol' bastard is up to something," he thought as he started away from the bluff. "I'd bet my pension he's gonna jump the reservation pretty soon."

As he drove across the ten-mile stretch toward Fort Sill, Sam was nagged by the vision of a frail old man atop a starving pony, riding toward a sunset following the flight of an eagle. If Sam remembered correctly, Chama would have to be well past seventy, now little more than a knot of wrinkled skin and bones, who bore little similarity to the fiery-eyed warrior who marched through the fort gate in chains twenty years before. Life at Fort Sill had taken its toll on Chama and the other Comanches. In their present state, they reminded Sam of caged animals, for they looked wild . . . until you looked at their eyes. The eyes told a sad story of defeat and hopelessness. Most of the Comanches and Kiowas were drunks, trading their few possessions and beef rations for whiskey. They were a pitiful lot, a ghostly reminder of what the reservation programs could do to free men. Only Chama, and two or three others that came to mind, still dressed in the old way and held to Comanche traditions.

A few miles from the rows of barracks and scattered shacks, they drove past the horse herd, about three hundred stunted ponies with ribs and hipbones sticking through thin hide. The drought had killed perhaps a hundred or more of the ponies this summer, a slow starvation with no grain or hay from the sutler's supplies. It was the Army's view that the horses were expendable. Cattle and sheep were fed just enough to keep them alive, while the little horses were allowed to starve to death. To a horseman like Sam, such treatment was just short of a crime.

Chama used sign language to tell Sam that he wanted to stop at the horse herd. Sam braked to a halt and switched off the motor.

Chama got out and walked toward the ponies. Sam sat, watching the multicolored horses sniff the air as Chama approached.

Chama began the guttural chant of the horse-breaker, a deep sound from his chest, soft and reassuring. A sorrel and white paint stallion nickered, and walked away from the others toward Chama, nostrils flared to catch the familiar scent of its master. Chama stopped, waited for the stallion to come near, saddened by the sight of his favorite pony, the gaunt frame and protruding ribs of a beautiful animal that was only a few weeks from death by starvation.

Like Chama, the pony was old and useless. It had been a gift from Chief Buffalo Hump, given on the day Chama's wife died, during the first winter at Fort Sill. Laughing Water had been too weak to survive the bitter cold with only one thin blanket. The coughing had begun suddenly, and in six days she departed on her spirit journey. Buffalo Hump had given Chama the colt, to lessen his sorrow. Laughing Water had been the last of Chama's four wives. The others died in the fusillade of bullets at Palo Duro as they reloaded his guns, helping him fight the soldiers. It was a beautiful colt, a powerful war horse. But eighteen taums had passed, and the paint stallion was now too old to make the long ride to Palo Duro carrying a rider.

The pony stood, feeling Chama's fingers rub the soft skin beneath its jaw. It would be a sad thing to leave the pony, but necessary. Chama must pick young horses for his escape, with dark colors so they would not be seen at night.

Chama heard Sam's footsteps behind him, and stopped the chant of the horse-breaker. The chant was a Comanche secret, enabling a Comanche to break wild horses in only a few days, unlike the *Tosi Tivo* way of saddling and gentling for weeks at a time. No white man would ever learn the chant from Chama, not even a *Tosi Tivo* with a good heart, like Sam Ault.

"They're in pretty bad shape," Sam said, gazing at the thin ponies. "Your old stud is about done-in. Tell you what . . . if you'll bring him out to my place, I'll see he gets some grain. I'll ask Tatum for permission, so you can bring him out to my barn. It ain't right, to starve horses like this. If I had the spare grain, I'd feed 'em all."

Chama was touched by the marshal's words, yet he could not allow himself to look on Sam's face. He must do nothing that might give his plans away, for the spirit shield might not be strong enough to keep the marshal from seeing his plan to escape. The marshal's medicine was very powerful. Had he not read Chama's heart back on the bluff? He knew Chama's thoughts without looking into his spirit. For a *Tosi Tivo,* his medicine was strong indeed.

Chama turned away from his pony and started for the car. The stallion followed him, nickering, breaking Chama's heart. He wanted to say farewell to his pony, but the marshal would understand his Comanche words. Thus there was no choice, but to turn his back on the gift for Laughing Water's departed spirit and walk away forever.

Sam cranked the car and started for the fort. Chama would not look back at the pony, he forced his thoughts to other things, the many things he must do with the coming of dark, to prepare for his escape toward Texas. He would visit Buffalo Hump and tell him of the spirit sign. The old chief lay dying in his bed, unable to lift his head from his blankets, his body filled with the *Tosi Tivo* coughing disease. Buffalo Hump would understand the power of the eagle sign, and his heart would be happy with the news that Powva had not abandoned the Comanches. He would know the message was clear for The People . . . they must follow Quinne to the west. If Buffalo Hump could rise, he would lead his people away from the fort to follow Quinne.

Then Chama must go to the others. There were but three among the Sata Exiponi that he could trust with his plan. Quahip, Poke, and Conas were the last of the Dog Soldiers strong enough in body and spirit to follow Chama. The other Comanches were too weak, or too crazy with *Boisah Pah,* to understand the spirit sign. Chama would not risk discovery by telling any of the others, for they might betray him to Agent Tatum for a bottle of crazy water.

Quahip was like Chama, once a brave warrior who was now crippled with age, almost seventy taums. Poke was much younger, perhaps fifty. As a young warrior, he had fought the soldiers with all his courage at Palo Duro. Conas was a giant among the Comanches, standing over six feet and four in his youth, until age bent his bones and enlarged his joints. He was now little more than a hulking skeleton, bent over with the pain in his bones as he hobbled among the shacks at the fort. But on a horse, he was still agile, reminding Chama of his days as a warrior when he leaned under his pony's neck, firing a rifle with deadly skill. Conas admitted to sixty taums, but Chama suspected he was much older.

It would be a powerful messasge to the other Comanches, if Chama and his followers made good their escape to Palo Duro. It would give them hope, and perhaps break the white man's spell on the rest of the Comanche bands. If the soldiers came back without Chama and the others, the rest might escape to follow them toward Texas, for they would understand the power in Chama's spirit sign.

Sam turned the car down a rutted lane between rows of sagging barracks and clapboard shacks, scattering chickens from the path of the machine, as he drove through the squalor of the Fort Sill Reservation to a shack at the end of the lane. Chama lived in a one-room cabin sitting away from the others near the gardens. Rows of dead corn plants rattled in a dry wind as Sam turned off the motor. The drought had ruined the small vegetable gardens, adding to the plight of the starving Indians.

"Bring your pony tomorrow. I'll clear it with Tatum."

Chama did not reply as he got out of the car.

"I know you're up to something, Chama. I figure you aim to make a run for it pretty soon. It'll kill you, old man. You can't make it very far. When Tatum catches you, he'll lock you up in the guardhouse. Things will be worse than they are now, if you live through it in the first place. Think about it. A man's life has gotta be worth something. Even livin' in this place is better than dyin'."

Chama got out of the car slowly, fixing his eyes on the last rays of sunlight along the western horizon.

"I am ready to die, *Tosi Tivo,*" Chama said softly. "For eighteen taums, my spirit has begged to begin the spirit journey. At this place, a Comanche can only wait for death. *Suvate* . . . that is all."

Sam sighed deeply, shaking his head.

"Bring the pony tomorrow. I'll fix it with Tatum."

Chama turned and walked to his shack, wishing he could say the words of thanks for the marshal's offer. But he could not risk any more talk with the marshal, for Chama feared he might betray his secret.

He heard the motor fade away as he lay down on his blankets to wait for dark. He must not allow his thoughts to remain on the pony, or Sam Ault, for there was much to be done in order to be ready for his escape.

Buffalo Hump must be told of the sign, and then the others . . . Quahip, Poke, and Conas. Then he must crawl beneath the shack and dig up the weapons, to clean the rifle and count his bullets and arrows. The first full moon was only two days away, and everything must be ready.

2

Chama sat cross-legged beside the pile of blankets, listening to the ragged breathing bubbling inside Buffalo Hump's chest. A lantern glowed in one corner of the shack, casting yellow light over the emaciated body, filling the sunken cheeks with shadow. It was a terrible sight, to see the great Kwahadie chief as he was now, little more than skin and bones. Even in the soft light, his eyes were dim, glazed with the nearness of death, his hands trembling as he waved his wife from the single room before Chama would speak.

"I bring a message of great importance," Chama whispered, "a message from Powva. Today, on the bluff west of the fort, I was given a spirit sign. Quinne flew above the bluff, circling over my head. Then he flew to the sun, toward the Palo Duro."

Buffalo Hump blinked.

"It was Quinne?" he gasped, strangling on the fluids in his chest. "You saw him well?"

"It was Quinne. I could see the white feathers of his tail as he flew over me."

21

Buffalo Hump coughed, a wet sound that warned of death.

"You must follow. It is the way of The People. Tell the others."

"They will not listen. Only a few of the old ones will come."

Buffalo Hump was silent a moment, sucking air into his failing lungs. Then he motioned for Chama to lean closer.

"You must take my grandson with you. He would follow in the path of his people. The white man's school has not changed his heart. He must go with you to Palo Duro."

Chama remembered the boy. Many times Chama had watched him ride his pony across the prairie beyond the fort, racing over the rough ground, riding like a true Comanche.

"He has but few taums. The soldiers will follow."

"He is fourteen. His name is Yellow Bull. The school has given him a white man's name . . . John Yellow Bull. He will be a strong warrior. He must go."

Chama did not like the idea. A fourteen-year-old boy would know nothing about fighting the soldiers, or how to hide his tracks on the journey.

"It is my last wish, Toyah Chama," the old chief whispered. "You must take him to Palo Duro. My spirit will be happy, knowing the boy is free of this terrible place."

Chama knew he could not refuse.

"I will take him with us. We leave with the full moon."

"Do not tell my old woman," the chief said sternly. "It will break her heart, but the boy must be free. Say nothing to her."

Buffalo Hump broke into a fit of coughing, then he lay still, his voice weaker as he spoke.

"When you come to Palo Duro, you must ride to the canyon, to the headwaters of the stream. Take the boy, and show him the clear water. Lie down and let him drink from the stream among the rocks. Let him taste the cool water. Then he will know what it means to be a free Comanche."

The chief's eyes closed. A final gurgling breath escaped his lips, then he departed on his spirit journey.

Chama sat beside Buffalo Hump's body for a long time without speaking, remembering the days of freedom in Pena Pah Canyon and the many battles he fought beside the Chief of the Kwahadies. No warrior among the Comanches had fought the blue-coats more bravely. Buffalo Hump was now at peace, and no longer a captive of the *Tosi Tivo*. His spirit was free at last of the stink at Fort Sill.

Chama left the shack as Buffalo Hump's wife began a mournful cry over the body of her husband. She was the last of his nine wives, for he had been a powerful chief, who could take as many women as he wanted. Buffalo Hump had outlived all but one of his wives, the wrinkled old woman who sang the *Nie Habbe Weichket* in the shack. Soon, her grief would be worsened by the departure of her grandson, but Chama had given his promise. The boy would go with them to Palo Duro.

Chama walked through the dark to tell the others, first Conas, then Quahip, and Poke. He said only that he had a message from Buffalo Hump, to come to his shack to hear the last words of their chief. Then he hurried to his shack, lit a lantern, and sat on the floor in silence, until all had arrived and gathered into a circle around the lantern.

"Buffalo Hump has departed on his spirit journey," Chama said finally, watching each face intently. "I spoke with him before he died. He gave me a message for his people."

Quahip leaned forward, the first to speak.

"What was his message?"

"He told me of his last wish," Chama replied, knowing this would add strength to their decision if they followed Chama. "I was given a spirit sign on the bluff. Buffalo Hump said the meaning was clear to all Comanches. Quinne flew above me, then he flew west toward the setting sun, toward the Palo Duro. Buffalo Hump told me I must follow the flight of Quinne, and lead the others back to the Pena Pah. He asked me to take his grandson, the boy called John Yellow Bull. It was the last wish of Buffalo Hump, before he departed to the spirit world."

Chama waited, allowing the full meaning of his spirit sign to reach the three men.

Conas stared at Chama, then at the lantern.

"For many years there have been no eagles in the skies above this place. It is powerful medicine, Chama. Quinne has come from Powva to show us the way."

Quahip agreed quickly.

"The words of Buffalo Hump must not be ignored. We must go, and go quickly. Powva has spoken. I am ready to leave this place."

Poke was the last to speak, his face dark.

"Are you certain it was Quinne you saw? Or was it the dreams of the peyote?"

Chama gazed into Poke's eyes.

"I could see the white feathers of his tail. Man-Who-Wears-The-Star saw him, too, and watched Quinne fly toward the sun."

Poke seemed uncertain.

"I have dreamed of Quinne many times, but in all the years at this stinking place, not one has come that my eyes could see."

Chama leaned closer, and lowered his voice.

"With the full moon, I will take two ponies and ride to the Palo Duro as Buffalo Hump wanted. Who will follow me?"

Conas and Quahip gave the sign of agreement at once. Poke sat a moment, as the others watched his face.

"The soldiers will come," he said finally. "They will not let us leave in peace. I am the only one among us who has a wife. Do I take my woman with me?"

Chama shook his head.

"The soldiers will come. It will be a long and difficult journey. We will take no women."

Poke stared at the lantern, thinking.

"It will be hard to leave the old woman," he said softly, "but I will go. It will be good to see our old home again."

"Say nothing to your woman," Chama whispered. "She must not warn the soldiers, or Tatum."

Poke gave the sign of agreement.

Chama looked at the other faces, and spoke in hushed tones.

"We must each select two good horses, dark, so they will not be seen at night. We will need weapons and waterskins. We will take what food we have, and kill fresh game on the trail. In two days, on the night of the full moon, we slip away to the cornfield when the others are asleep. Tell no one about our plan. No one. Some will trade our lives for a bottle of *Boisah Pah.*"

Conas shrugged.

"I have no weapon."

"I have an old pistol," Quahip whispered, "but only four bullets. We need many more to fight the bluecoats."

"I have a rifle," Poke said, "and many bullets, tied in a bundle of deerskin. When we first came here, I buried the gun near the garden. Every spring, when Tatum plows the field, I watch, hoping he will not find them. I will dig them up tomorrow night and clean the rifle."

"I, too, have a rifle," Chama said, "buried under the floor of this shack. With three guns, we can fight the soldiers."

"What about the boy?" Conas asked darkly. "Can we trust him not to warn the soldiers?"

"I will talk with him," Chama replied, "but I will wait for the day when we leave. I gave Buffalo Hump my promise that I would take the boy with us. I will pick two ponies for him, but say nothing to him until we are ready to ride."

"Where will we hide our ponies?" Quahip asked, "so that no one will find them?"

Chama had already decided what would be done about the horses.

"We will take them to the narrow canyon east of the fort, and hide them in the tall trees. When the soldiers find the tracks, they will think we have ridden east. We will ride the canyon rim, over the rocks to hide our

26

tracks. No one will think to look west toward the Palo Duro."

For another hour they talked and planned, discussing waterskins and things they would need. When the talk ended, they left one at a time, slipping quietly among the night shadows to their homes.

Chama was satisfied. Like himself, the three Sata Exiponi were pleased with the spirit sign. They were eager to start the long ride west. Quinne had brought powerful medicine on his flight above the reservation, and the gift of hope that they might once again live as free men on the open plains.

Only the problem of the boy troubled Chama, as he tried to drift toward sleep, his belly full of dried beef after four days of fasting on the bluff. One so young, with no experience as a warrior, could slow them down. Fourteen taums was a very short time, not enough to learn the lessons of a warrior, but it would have to be enough. Chama had given his promise . . . and the boy would go with them.

An hour before dawn, Chama was among the ponies in the corrals west of the agency office, the pens where the workhorses were kept and fed by Tatum. Most were young colts, two- and three-year-olds, strong enough to pull the plows and wagons used in the gardens, a thing demanded by Tatum of all the Indians at the fort as a part of his program to teach farming. It was a humiliating experience for the Comanches, to take their war-horses and harness them to the plows. The ponies fought the harness and chains in the

27

beginning years of Tatum's experiment. Chama remembered those times as he examined the white collar marks on the withers of the ponies; it was the white man's brand on all the descendants of the horse herd they brought with them from Palo Duro.

With the blade of a kitchen knife, Chama walked among the ponies, selecting a bay gelding and a brown mare. He cut two notches in the mane of each pony, his mark from the old days that identified his horses. Quahip, Poke, and Conas would come to the corrals to mark their own brands on the ponies they would ride.

Chama picked two dark geldings for the boy, cutting the mark of Buffalo Hump in their tails. Tomorrow night they would slip the ten horses out of the corrals, and hide them at the back of the canyon. The soldiers would not miss ten ponies from the hundred or so in the pens.

As dawn broke to the east, he hurried back to his shack and opened the bundle of weapons on his sleeping blankets. His bow and ten dogwood arrows were still in usable shape, even after eighteen taums beneath the hut. His Spencer needed oil, and two of the seven cartridges were badly corroded, but the rifle would fire after a good cleaning. His weapons, like those of Quahip and Poke, had come to Fort Sill under the robes of the Comanche women, tied in rawhide slings beneath their skirts on the march from Palo Duro. The soldiers were too stupid to search the women's robes, or too lazy.

And last among Chama's hidden possessions was the fencing tool, the wire cutter Chama had stolen from the agency store. He had seen the barbed wire fences crossing the western boundaries of the reservation, and watched carefully as the soldiers cut the wires with the tool. He had known, from the beginning, that he would need such a tool for his escape. Ponies could not jump the high wire fences of the *Tosi Tivo*.

Chama oiled the rifle and worked the mechanism, satisfied that the old Spencer would fire. Then he tied the bundle and hid it under his blankets before he began his prayers to the four spirits: the sun, mother earth, the moon, and the stars. But before he finished his prayers, he heard soft footsteps outside his door. He opened his eyes, wondering who would come at such an early hour, and was relieved to see Quahip standing under the shade of his porch.

Chama went out and glanced quickly around the rows of shacks, concerned by Quahip's visit, hoping there was no trouble. All night, as he slept fitfully—dreaming about Quinne and his escape toward Palo Duro—he worried that his plan might be discovered, that one of the three Sata Exiponi might talk to some of the others and reveal their escape.

"Why did you come?" Chama asked, searching his old friend's face.

"To make talk," Quahip replied, settling against Chama's porch. "So many dreams came in my sleep . . . so many good dreams about Pena Pah, and the Palo Duro. Then, in my dream I saw the soldiers, Chama. Many soldiers, coming behind us like the dark cloud of a storm. They will come after us. I saw them clearly in my dream."

Chama squatted against the wall of his hut, watching the activity begin in the early hours, the children leaving for the white man's school, and the young men starting toward the dry fields to pick what was left

29

of the corn.

"It will not be easy," Chama sighed, thinking of words that might reassure Quahip. It was unwise to ignore the dream, for it was often Powva's plan to show The People what lay ahead with images sent while a man slept. All too often the message in a dream came to pass, something any warrior understood after living the dream in battle. "Tatum must send the soldiers after us, to keep the others from leaving. We must ride hard, and keep our eyes on the trail behind us. I, too, was troubled by dreams last night. It is Powva's way of preparing us for the danger ahead. With the power of Quinne to guide us, we will see the Pena Pah again. It is the will of Powva that we be free of this place. He sent Quinne to guide us."

Quahip agreed with a shake of his head.

"I saw the canyon in my dream, Chama. I saw many deer, and so many wild turkey, they covered the ground like a robe. The waters in the stream were clear. It was my happiest dream in many taums. I could smell the clean air. There was no stink of death. I woke up with tears in my eyes, like some foolish woman."

Chama let a silent moment pass, watching the chickens scratch in the dry ground, thinking how foolish it was for Tatum to give the Comanches and Kiowas his chickens. No one would eat the eggs, even the lazy Kiowas, and it was forbidden to kill the birds to eat the meat. Chicken eggs had a terrible taste. The small children threw them at each other, adding the smell of rotten eggs to the stink of the overcrowded reservation.

"We will make it to the canyon," Chama said finally. "The soldiers will come, and they will make us fight,

30

but we will make it to Pena Pah. We must be strong, like in the days before the treaty, and fight if they give us no choice. If I am chosen by Powva to die in battle, then it will be His plan. I am ready to die fighting, rather than spend another taum at this place. To die bravely in battle is better than sitting here, waiting for death."

Chama glanced at Quahip, thinking how old and tired his friend seemed, his muscles turned to sagging skin, his face a tangle of webbed lines hanging loosely from his skull. Once, he was among the best fighters of the Kwahadies, taking many scalps and fighting fearlessly from the back of his pony. He still wore the deerskin leggings and beaded shirt, like Chama, refusing the loose cotton pants and shirts given at the agency store. In his heart, he was still a Comanche. He would fight hard, if the soldiers came after them. He was still a warrior in spirit.

"I saw death, Chama," he said hoarsely, gazing at the morning sky. "In my dream, I saw death among the Sata Exiponi. Some of us will die, trying to reach Pena Pah."

Chama did not reply for a moment, thinking about Quahip's dream.

"If death comes," Chama said finally, "I will be ready for my spirit journey. Living at this place is no different than death. I am ready to die."

Quahip turned and met Chama's eyes.

"I too, am ready for the spirit journey. Let the soldiers come. I will kill many, before they send their bullets into my heart. *Suvate.*"

Quahip stood up, standing tall in the shadows of the porch. Then he walked away toward his hut, his shoulders thrown back as he scattered chickens from his path. Chama noticed a difference in his walk, for it now seemed that Quahip moved with the easy strides of a much younger man.

Chama leaned back against the cabin wall, dozing, remembering the headwaters of the canyon stream where he promised to take John Yellow Bull. In his dream, the water was alive with fish, clear and cool to the tongue, gurgling over rocks as it swept past him toward the end of the canyon. It was a wonderful dream, so real he could feel the grass beneath his feet and the scent of fresh air in his nose. Like Quahip, he dreamed of wild turkey and deer, so plentiful no arrow could miss its mark. Once, in the years before the *Tosi Tivo* came, the Pena Pah was like his dream, a place of peace and beauty where the Kwahadies had everything they needed. Chama was certain the canyon would be as they had left it, a place where wild game and clear water provided all any man could ever want. It would be worth any price to see the Pena Pah again, no matter how many soldiers followed, or how difficult the journey might be.

A chicken squawked, fluttering its wings, awakening Chama from his dream. He looked down the lane past the rows of shacks, and his heart came to a stop. Agent Ike Tatum walked toward him, looking straight at Chama as he drew near. At once, Chama knew something was wrong.

"Hot, ain't it?" Tatum said, as he stopped in front of the porch.

Chama did not reply, or look at Tatum's face. Of all the *Tosi Tivo* he had fought, he hated the Indian Agent above them all. When he first came to Fort Sill, Chama dreamed of slipping through Tatum's window at night and slicing off his scalp. No man had brought more suffering to the Comanches than Ike Tatum. The short little man with orange-red hair hated all Indians, reserving a special dislike for Comanches. For eighteen taums, Tatum had done everything he could to make life miserable for his prisoners at the fort.

"I sent Sam Ault to pick you up yesterday," Tatum began. "If you wander away again like that, I'll have you chained up in the guardhouse on bread and water. Don't leave again, old man. Is that understood?"

Chama understood most of Tatum's words, but could not bring himself to answer. Chama only shook his head, the white man's way of saying yes.

"You're nothing but an old troublemaker," Tatum continued. "I'll be glad when some of the old bastards like you are dead and gone. You make trouble for the others. Buffalo Hump is dead, finally. Maybe you'll get your ass to the happy hunting ground heap pretty quick, too," he said, chuckling. "One other thing . . . Sam asked for my permission to let you bring your horse out to his place, so he could feed it. I told him it didn't make a damn bit of difference to me. From the looks of you, I figure you're too old to ride a horse in the first place, but if you want to take the horse, I'll send a trooper along just to be damn sure you come back. Don't forget, old man, I meant what I said about runnin' off to that bluff. If you do it again, I'll keep you in chains the rest of your life. I can't let you set a bad example for the rest of 'em."

Tatum walked off without waiting for a reply, scattering his chickens, muttering to himself. For a fleeting moment Chama gave thought to unwrapping the

Spencer and sending a bullet into Tatum, but the lure of freedom in the Palo Duro kept him where he sat. It would be better to escape Tatum's soldiers, and be rid of the stink at Fort Sill forever. If he killed the agent, they would only send another, while Chama sat in chains inside the guardhouse.

Chama closed his eyes and dreamed of the canyon again. It was a way of preparing himself for the hardships of the escape ahead. Nothing must stop them, no matter how many wire fences he had to cut, or how many soldiers Tatum sent after them. Escape was all that mattered, to be free of the men like Tatum and the blue-coat soldiers.

At midnight the four sat cross-legged around the lantern in Chama's shack, watching as Poke displayed the box of fifty shells on the blanket. Some were too badly corroded to fire, lying for so long in the earth near the gardens. His Spencer lay near his feet, rusted but usable with a fresh layer of oil.

"It is enough," Chama said softly, as Poke wrapped the skin around his weapons. Quahip added his old Navy Colt to the bundle, and four percussion caps. Six lead balls were packed in the firing chambers, but only four had caps to fire them. Chama put the bundle under his sleeping blankets with his own weapons, then he leaned forward, and spoke in hushed tones.

"We must go quietly to move the ponies. I will take Poke and Quahip. Conas, you stand outside and watch the soldier rooms. If something is wrong, give the call of the owl twice."

They left the shack silently, one at a time, moving

among the shadows as the moon cast silver light on the dry ground. After one more day they would have a full moon to guide them, to light their passage westward.

The three made their way carefully to the corrals. Quahip opened the gate as Chama slipped a war bridle—a single rawhide rein with a loop for the pony's jaw—on the chosen mounts. He led them outside, handing each one to Quahip and Poke, until the ten were caught.

Chama took four ponies and led the way wide of the fort, keeping to the deepest shadows. They led the ponies over a mile before they entered the box canyon, winding through a forest of live oak and elm to a place at the back of the canyon, where the sheer limestone wall made a shelter for the ponies. They hobbled each pony with a jaw rein, then the three left at a trot toward the reservation. Not a word was said among them, for none was needed. It was all a part of their training as a Dog Soldier, a drill to make ready for war that they had practiced a hundred times before.

Soundlessly, they split apart to return to their homes, and to wait for their final day to pass as prisoners at Fort Sill. If nothing went wrong, they would leave at midnight, after the soldiers were asleep. It would be six or seven hours before anyone would find them missing, enough time to put better than fifty miles between themselves and the *Tosi Tivo* enemy.

3

Late in the afternoon, as Chama sat on his porch remembering the landmarks they would follow toward Texas, he glanced up at the sounds of children. As the school day ended, several boys came walking through the rows of shacks, carrying books. Among them was John Yellow Bull, a slender, hard-muscled youth with close-cropped hair, cut in the white man's fashion like all the other children attending the school. It was the white man's law that all Indian children attend the agency classes, to learn the *Tosi Tivo* language and to learn to read from books. All but the eldest of the Comanche children had been born on the reservation. A few were only infants, strapped to their mother's backs during the fight at Palo Duro.

Chama let the boy go inside Buffalo Hump's hut, before he got up and walked to the open doorway. Buffalo Hump's widow peered out at him, her face painted black in the Comanche way of mourning a loved one, even though the soldiers had come for the body the day before.

"I want talk with the boy," Chama said. Moments later John Yellow Bull came out on the porch, a question in his eyes.

"Come. I have a message for you, Yellow Bull."

Chama had spoken to the boy in Comanche, wondering if he knew the language of his people.

"I am called Taoyo," the boy replied in Comanche, as he came down from the porch to follow Chama.

They walked some distance before Chama spoke again, waiting until they entered the gardens, to be away from listening ears.

"I have a message from your grandfather," Chama said softly, searching the black eyes of the boy. "Buffalo Hump told me you would follow the old ways, the way of your people."

Taoyo gave the sign of agreement, evidence that he had learned many of the old ways from his grandfather.

For a moment, Chama wondered how he should begin. He was taking a chance, for if the boy warned the soldiers, it would mean the guardhouse for himself and the others. All day he worried about the outcome of his talk with John Yellow Bull, what would happen when he told the boy about their plan.

"It was your grandfather's last wish that you be free of this place, Taoyo. Before your grandfather departed on his spirit journey, he asked me to take you away from the reservation, to go back to the place of our forefathers in Texas."

Chama watched the boy's face intently, trying to read the feelings behind the dark, questioning eyes.

"I would go willingly," Taoyo replied, "but it is for-

38

bidden to leave Fort Sill. My grandfather told me many stories about the Palo Duro, and the canyon called Pena Pah. This is a place for pigs, and Kiowas."

Chama smiled at the boy's words, spoken like a true Comanche.

"If you could leave very soon, even if the danger was great, would you go?"

Suddenly, there was recognition in Taoyo's eyes. He understood why Chama called him to the gardens.

"I would be proud to leave with a brave warrior such as you, Toyah Chama. There would be no danger. My grandfather told me the stories of your courage in battle. You are Chief of the Sata Exiponi. The soldiers could not defeat you. It would be a great honor to ride with you to Palo Duro."

Chama knew at once that the boy would not betray his plan. Taoyo reminded Chama of the young Kwahadies of long ago, begging to go on their first war party, eyes alight with excitement.

"It was the last wish of Buffalo Hump. I gave my promise that I would take you with me to Texas. Come to my shack tonight, before the moon comes to the sky. Say nothing to your grandmother, or to anyone. We leave tonight."

"I must catch my pony from the herd. Where will I hide the pony?"

"Two ponies have already been chosen for you. Come before the moon, and say nothing to anyone."

Taoyo gave the sign of agreement, turning on his heels to run toward his shack. Chama watched him go, feeling good about his talk with the boy. In his heart, Taoyo was a Comanche, in spite of his clipped hair and white man's clothing. He spoke the tongue as well as any of the old ones. Buffalo Hump had taught his grandson the ways of his people.

Chama went to his shack to lie down, trying to sleep. The rest would be badly needed in the days ahead, with the soldiers pressing hard from behind. But sleep would not come, only more of the visions of Palo Duro and Pena Pah. For the first time in many taums, he found himself looking forward to the beginning of a new day, riding his pony away from this reservation.

Long before the moon came over the horizon, Chama saw a shadow move outside his door. His ears had not warned him of anyone's footsteps. Chama got up and crept to the opening, surprised to see the boy standing a few yards away, the first to come. He motioned the boy inside, noticing a change in Taoyo's appearance as he walked past Chama into the shack. He was dressed in an old deerskin shirt that bore the beaded sign of Buffalo Hump, a pair of leggings and moccasins, with a waterskin slung over one shoulder. Buffalo Hump's garments were too large for the boy, but it was plain Taoyo wore them proudly as he squatted on the floor beside the lantern.

"I am ready, Toyah Chama," the boy whispered in Comanche.

"We must wait for the others. Be silent, and ask Powva for strong medicine on our journey."

First Conas, then Quahip arrived on silent moccasined feet to sit by the lantern. Last came Poke, carrying food and his waterskin. Without a word Chama took the bundles of weapons from beneath his blankets and handed them to the others. Then he took his water-skin and a small bundle of dried beef, before he turned off the lantern and walked to the doorway.

For several minutes Chama stood, listening to the sounds from the dark reservation, waiting until his senses told him all was clear. This was the one moment he dreaded as he planned every detail of their escape. If anyone had learned of their plans and sent a warning to Tatum, the soldiers would be waiting for them to slip away from the fort. The greatest danger lay in getting past the soldiers' quarters without being seen. It would take all the cunning they possessed, to move quietly without alerting the dogs or the sentries.

Chama stepped into the shadows beside his shack and crept to the edge of the cornfield. Off in the distance a dog barked, then fell silent. Chama waited, listening to the pounding of his heart, the Spencer held ready in the crook of his arm.

The first rays of silvery moonlight bathed the barren ground behind the corrals. Crossing the open stretches toward the canyon, they would be in plain sight for anyone who watched from the agency office. It was a chance they must take, for there was no other way to reach the ponies.

Silently Chama led the way through the dry corn plants, sweeping everything in their path with a careful look. They passed the corrals and stopped, listening to the heavy silence around them.

Chama lifted his rifle and broke into a trot across the moonlit prairie, leading the others at a fast pace away from the reservation. Conas struggled to keep up on his

41

painful joints, as they ran past the rows of soldiers' quarters. A dog barked somewhere behind them, the sound much too distant to be a warning to the soldiers.

They covered the mile without incident. Conas gasped for breath, his ankles and knees throbbing with pain when they entered the first sheltering of trees at the entrance to the canyon. They ran to the hobbled ponies and untied the rawhide reins, breathing hard from the length of their run. Chama showed Taoyo his mounts, then he tied his waterskin and food bundle to the back of one pony and swung up on the pony's withers. He gathered the rein on his spare mount, and waited for the others to climb on their ponies and tie their gear in place.

Chama reined his pony south, moving along the base of the limestone cliff, until he found the narrow niche leading to the top. The ponies scrambled for footing on the sheer climb, often stumbling over fallen rock and loose stones, until Chama wound his way to the rim of the canyon.

He waited, watching the others ride out of the niche to the edge of the cliff. Poke came last up the twisting trail, leading his spare pony, with the Spencer hung from his shoulder on a rawhide thong.

Moving slowly, picking the rockiest ground, Chama walked his pony along the rim, listening for the sounds of pursuit as he led the others west. Conas rode easily behind Chama, then came the boy, followed by Quahip. Poke came last, ready to defend the rear of the party with his box of fifty bullets. At the front, Chama was armed with his rifle and the bow. Quahip carried his pistol stuck in his belt. Only Conas and Taoyo had no weapons.

Finding a slab of smooth limestone, Chama swung south to ride around the reservation, leaving no tracks as the little unshod hooves carried the riders soundlessly over the rock.

It was the fall of the white man's year 1908. For almost twenty years, the United States Army and The Bureau of Indian Affairs held all the American Indian tribes at peace on federal reservations. Most Americans had forgotten the Indian troubles of the past century. But with the flight of a bald eagle over Fort Sill, Oklahoma, old memories returned, as a party of Kwahadie Comanches broke free of their reservation, riding into a century that had already begun to fill with automobiles, highways, and barbed wire fences. A page of America's past came unexpectedly into the future, spreading alarm among the quiet settlements of western Oklahoma and Texas.

Sam Ault entered Ike Tatum's office amid the flurry of activity, uniformed soldiers hurrying across the fort compound with saddled horses and loaded rifles. Sam walked to the back of the agency and entered Tatum's private office, glancing at a pair of well-dressed men and a woman scribbling furiously on a notepad as Ike Tatum addressed the group.

"So you see," Tatum said gravely, "what we have here is a very dangerous situation. The renegades are Comanches, and our report indicates they may have broken into our armory to steal rifles. These Indians are armed and dangerous . . . I want to stress that point to your newspapers. Of all the Indian tribes in America, none of them are as bad as Comanches,

43

particularly this group that escaped Fort Sill last night. We keep records on the worst of these people, and the ones we're talking about have a long history of murder and torture. Some of these men scalped hundreds of innocent settlers in Texas before the army captured them. It would be no understatement to say that these Kwahadie Comanches are the most brutal savages on earth. No man, woman, or child in Oklahoma will be safe until these men are captured. Right now, we aren't sure how many escaped, but if I had to take a guess, it would be somewhere close to fifty."

The woman spoke as she jotted notes on her pad.

"What can you tell our readers about the measures the army is taking to round up these Indians?"

"We've sent out horseback patrols, and will put more men into the field within the hour. We think the Comanches are headed east, toward Lawton. You can tell your readers that if anyone sights these Indians, they should contact Fort Sill at once. I talked with the sheriff at Lawton this morning. He's organizing a posse. We think they're headed toward Lawton."

Sam could not believe his ears. Without being told, he knew old Chama was one of the escapees. But fifty? It did not seem possible that fifty Comanches would follow Chama from the reservation.

One of the reporters stopped writing and formed a question.

"I seem to remember that the Comanche Chief is a half-breed white man named Quannah Parker. Is he the one who is leading this Indian revolt?"

Tatum shook his head, glancing at Sam.

"Chief Quannah Parker doesn't live on the reservation. He owns a house in Cache. I doubt if he even knows about this war party. I've had no problems with Quannah . . . probably because he's half-white, like you say. We think the Indian who is responsible for all this is an old troublemaker called Toyah Chama. In English, this name means 'the squealing pig,' or something like that."

"Voice of the Wild Boar," Sam interrupted softly.

"Whatever," Tatum snapped, tossing Sam a glare. "In any case, we feel sure Chama is the one who led the revolt. In his younger days, he was the worst murderer of the bunch. Our files contain brutal accounts of how he tortured and mutilated innocent white farmers, even women and children. You can put that in your story if you wish. The leader of this revolt is a crazed killer of women and children. We've got the reports in our files."

"Spell his name for us," the woman said, her pen ready above her notepad.

Tatum spelled the Comanche name slowly, reading from a list atop his desk.

"And my name is Ike Tatum. I'm the Indian Agent here at Fort Sill, if you need that for your story."

Sam shook his head, gazing out a window at the mounted troops assembling in the compound. Oddly, Tatum seemed to be enjoying the furor over Chama's escape, adding unnecessary and inaccurate details about Chama and the Comanches. Tatum knew little about Indians, and less about Comanches. Twenty years as Indian Agent at Fort Sill had done nothing to broaden his interest in his Indian captives. He still understood only three or four words of the Indians' tongue.

Tatum got up from his desk, dismissing the three

45

reporters as he walked to the office door. The reporters left hurriedly, climbing into sputtering cars to rush the story to Lawton, Tulsa, and Cache. Sam knew Tatum's version of things would make big headlines in western Oklahoma, sending fear into the hearts of readers who lived close to Fort Sill. If, as Tatum said, there were a party of fifty armed Comanches on the warpath again, it *would* be cause for alarm. But Sam doubted that fifty warriors had followed Chama from the reservation. Chama was no longer a fighter. If anything, he was headed for his old stomping ground in the Texas Panhandle to escape the misery of the reservation. Something about the way the old man refused to look at him, the other day at the bluff, made Sam suspect that this was simply an escape from the fort to freedom. Likely, only a few were willing to follow him, fearing Tatum's reprisal. Before, Chama had tried to talk some of the others into running away, and failed to find a single follower. For some reason, the old man would not try such a feat alone.

Sam took a chair opposite Tatum's desk.

"Tell me what happened. How many are missing?"

Tatum took a seat and folded his hands on his desk.

"We don't know yet how many are gone. Chama, and several others are missing from a roll call this morning. We found tracks in the canyon east of the fort. A patrol counted the tracks of about fifty horses, headed east toward Lawton."

Sam pulled off his stetson and ran a hand absently through his thinning hair.

"I came as soon as I got your message. The trooper made it sound like every Indian at Fort Sill was gone."

Tatum shrugged, watching the movement of troops

beyond his window.

"Some of the young cavalrymen get excited. They're too young to know anything about fighting Indians. It's my guess they're about to get their first chance. I'm through playing games with ol' Chama and his kind. A few of those old bastards keep stirring things up, making it hard on the ones who are trying to follow orders and do what we tell 'em to do. I have the order to shoot them on sight. It's my duty, Sam. I can't let a few rotten apples spoil the whole barrel. My job's on the line, too. If those Comanches lift any scalps in Lawton, I'll get a transfer to some place worse than Fort Sill, if such a place exists."

Sam sighed, dropping his hat on his head.

"I'll go have a look at the tracks. Maybe I can find out which way they headed."

"My guess is Lawton. Closest place to kill white people."

"Did they really break in and steal rifles?"

Tatum avoided Sam's eyes.

"Can't say for sure. We're taking an inventory. Probably know in a day or two."

Sam studied the office wall where a picture hung, of Ike Tatum standing in front of the agency office with dignitaries from Washington, taken on the day the new facilities were dedicated over twenty years ago. Most men in federal service were promoted in that length of time. Sam guessed that Ike Tatum knew he was stuck here at Fort Sill, probably until his retirement.

As Sam got up, the office door flew open. A uniformed officer came smartly into the office with a clipboard in his hands. Sam recognized the soldier as Major Walter Townsend, Post Commander of the detail at Fort Sill.

Townsend nodded to Sam before he addressed Tatum.

"We've come up with a list of eight names so far. There's the one called Toyah Chama, of course, and three more men about the same age. One is Conas, the big one who limps, and then Quahip, and one named Poke. His wife is missing, too . . . doesn't answer a roll call, a woman named Salope. Buffalo Hump's wife is gone, an old woman called Pohawcut. We're checking to see if this is related to the escape. The woman could be out at the cemetery to visit the body of her husband. Her grandson is missing, too, a boy named John Yellow Bull, but I doubt if these two are involved in the revolt. We know there are more, but so far I've only got eight names."

Tatum gave Sam a wary look.

"We found fifty sets of tracks, Major. Keep checking."

Townsend turned on his heel and started for the door.

"If I were you, Major," Sam said, "I'd send a patrol west, toward the old Kirk Ranch headquarters. Unless I miss my guess, you'll find a handful of Comanches right about now, tryin' to find a way around all that barbed wire fence west of the creek."

Townsend looked at Tatum, a question on his face.

"Might as well," Tatum sighed. "Marshal Ault knows more about these damn Indians than the rest of us. But keep the patrols riding back and forth toward Lawton. I say they're headed east to burn farms and lift scalps. I guess we'll have to wait and see who's right."

Sam walked to the door, jerking a thumb toward the window.

"I'm afraid you're gonna be disappointed with this revolt," Sam replied tonelessly. "My guess is, this is only a few of the old ones trying to get back home before they die. I'll go have a look at the tracks, but I'm pretty sure what I'm gonna find. Chama ain't lookin' for a fight, only a clear path to Texas."

Sam walked out, leaving the two men without waiting for a reply. As Sam cranked the Star touring car, Major Townsend came out and snapped an order to the mounted patrol. Before Sam got the engine started, eighty troopers galloped away to the west in a cloud of dust, following a young captain at the head of the column toward the western boundary of the reservation.

Sam drove over the bumpy ground to the box canyon where a patrol had reported the tracks, he switched off the motor at the edge of a stand of live oak. His thoughts were filled with visions of Chama, riding a skinny paint stallion, to a fence made from strands of barbed wire . . . stopping, not knowing what to do about the white man's barrier. Fences had come to the plains long after Chama's confinement on the reservation. The old Indian would not know what to do about the fences, unable to jump a pony over the wires.

Sam climbed painfully from the seat and walked through the trees, taking mincing steps as the arthritis in his ankles and knees protested under his weight. Walking a quarter-mile into the forest, he came to the south wall of the canyon and looked down at the hoofprints and horse droppings littering the canyon floor.

It was easy to see how an uninitiated observer might mistake so many tracks for a big group of horses. Sam walked about, studying the ground carefully, until he found the niche in the canyon wall leading to the rim.

Slowly, a step at a time, he followed the hoofprints upward, pausing now and then to read the sign, practicing an art he had not used for many years.

At the top he found what he expected . . . the tracks of ten or eleven unshod ponies turning west over the rocks along the canyon rim, soon lost to the untrained eye as the ponies crossed slabs of limestone. Most people, even experienced trackers, would have lost the tiny scratch of a hoof, so faint in the limestone it was only a trace of the passing of an eight-hundred-pound Indian pony carrying a rider. It was all the proof he needed that the mounted men were Comanches. No other Indian on the plains could accomplish such a feat, making the tracks of a horse disappear in thin air. The Comanches were unequalled in vanishing tactics, another reason it had taken the cavalry so many years to corner them in battle. A part of the feat came from the ponies themselves, tough little mustangs selectively bred for hard hooves and stamina, beyond anything the soldiers could buy. Chasing a horseback Comanche was akin to following a prairie wind, never quite catching up, but always close enough for one more try.

"You old fox," Sam muttered, gazing at the western horizon. "I knew damn well you were up to something this time. You finally did it. I bet it was that eagle done the trick. Big medicine, you sly old bastard. It ain't gonna be easy to find you, now that you've got eight or ten hours out in front."

Sam wondered about the missing guns, as he gazed

at the sun overhead. If Chama and his men had rifles, he would put up one hell of a fight if he was cornered. The old man knew he was dying, and had said so back at the bluff. He would think nothing of killing a few soldiers in order to escape the reservation, for the chance to see the Palo Duro canyon again. He wanted to die in the land of his forefathers, and would die in the attempt if anyone pushed him. It seemed he had finally convinced a handful of others, probably only eight or nine, judging by the tracks. A bunch of old experienced fighters like Quahip and Conas would make the soldiers pay dearly if it came down to a fight. If, as Tatum said, the Comanches had stolen rifles.

What old Chama did not realize, was how much the country west of Fort Sill had changed since he had arrived here eighteen years before. What was once open rangeland was now filled with wire fences, and roads heavy with traffic. Western Oklahoma and the Texas panhandle had been settled since Chama's time, with new towns springing up all over the place to block his path. Chama might not recognize the trail he hoped to follow, lost in the mazes of fences and farms; the old landmarks were gone, as farmers plowed the prairies and built their homes and barns. As word spread of Tatum's Comanche uprising through newspapers and along the miles of telegraph and telephone lines, Chama could face armed posses of terrified farmers, who believed Tatum's stories about mutilated women and children. Chama, and a few old Indians like him, would not stand a chance against so many.

Sam left the rim and walked back down the trail to his car, surprised at himself for the odd mixture of feelings rattling around inside his head. It was the army's job, and Tatum's, to go after the Comanches. Yet it would be a sad moment, when news came back that a patrol—or an armed posse of farmers—killed the old Indians in a gun battle, probably near the first fence Chama could not cross. As U.S. Marshal for the Oklahoma Territory, he spent a big part of his career rounding up renegade Indians, but strangely, Sam found himself hoping Chama made good on his escape. Chama, and the other old warriors, were harmless if left alone to ride back to Texas. It seemed a shame to have half the population of Oklahoma bristling with guns in an effort to stop them. Tatum's version of the Comanche uprising was a tragic variation from the truth found in the ponies' tracks. As soon as the newspapers picked up the story, the handful of feeble old Indians would face a fate no different than ducks at a shooting gallery.

"Too bad," Sam thought, as he cranked the motor and climbed in the seat. Sam liked Chama. It was more a keen respect for how long the old man had held fast to his old beliefs, even in the face of the hopelessness of life on the reservation. For many years, Chama came alone to the bluff west of the fort to pray to his god for a sign of hope. It had taken almost twenty years before his prayers seemed repaid, as the eagle flew over his head. In his heart, the old Indian knew his faith was answered. It made no difference that the dry year might have forced the eagle to range farther for food. To him, it was the answer to prayer, a message filled with hope for a dying man.

Sadly, the eagle would turn out to be a death sentence for Chama and his followers, as they tried to relive a past that was gone forever. It would be a sad thing indeed to learn that a bullet ended Chama's hopes, before he made it back to Texas. The Comanches would not make it through four hundred miles of changed land to Palo Duro. But Sam knew they would try.

He drove to his farm north of the reservation, admiring his saddle horses grazing on a mound of hay near the barn. The sight reminded Sam of Chama's old paint pony, a sad creature that was not strong enough in its present condition to carry Chama for more than a few miles. The pony and the old Indian were both too old and weak to stand any chance of escaping the troopers. The more Sam thought about it, the more tragic the whole affair seemed.

Sam spoke to his wife as she set plates for supper. He told Clara about the Indians, and his suspicion that the revolt was only a few old men trying to make their way back to their ancestral home.

Clara heard the sorrow in her husband's voice, and thought about how much he had changed in the last few years.

"You're becoming a soft-hearted old cuss, Mr. Ault. Time was you'd have gone for weeks, looking for those runaway Indians until the tracks played out. Sounds to me like you want these Comanches to get where they're going. I do believe you've gone soft on me, Marshal."

Clara gave him a smile as she poured iced tea.

"The way those Indians are treated is a downright shame," she continued, busying herself with their supper. "Looks to me like some of the higher-ups in Washington should be notified about conditions out here. I've kept dogs better fed than Tatum does those Indians. Can't say as I blame any of them for wanting

53

to run away."

Sam nodded agreement from his easy chair.

"You're always right, aren't you, woman? In forty-six years, I can't remember a time when you admitted to being wrong about things. It's true, the conditions at Fort Sill are pretty bad. I suppose they've always been this way, only I didn't bother to give them a close look. Still, it's the law that the Indians have to stay on the reservations. I've spent my whole career enforcing the laws, Clara. I can't just stop now, because I don't like this particular incident. But I have to admit that I hope these old men get away from Tatum's cavalry, at least for a little while. One of them, an old fellow named Chama, deserves a better way to die than rotting away at Fort Sill. He's different, still a proud old warrior who believes his god intends to set him free and show him the way home. All the rest of the Comanches have given up, but not ol' Chama. He won't let go. I gotta hand it to any man who can believe in something for so many years."

Clara left the table and walked over to him, placing a hand gently against his cheek.

"Time you quit this job, husband. You're getting soft in your old age. Just a few more months, and then you can hand things over to Tom. I'll be glad to see the day come. Dr. Roberts says the arthritis will only get worse as time goes by. Time you quit trying to do a young man's job."

Sam got up, wincing with the pain in his knees, and joined Clara for supper.

"Tonight I'll rub some of the salve on your knees," she said, while she filled his plate. "Maybe it'll help take your mind off those Indians."

A mounted trooper stood his horse beyond the gate into Sam's front yard, foam was clinging to the winded animal's neck from a hard ride, as the soldier spoke to the marshal.

"We found them, sir. Just where you said they would be, at the Kirk Ranch fence. We've got them pinned down with rifle fire. Major Townsend said to come get you right away, so you can talk to them for us."

Sam left the porch and waved to the trooper, cranking the car while he told himself how right he had been from the beginning. The Comanches made it to the first fence in their path, and could find no way around it.

He climbed in the sputtering car and drove west as the sun lowered in front of him. Sam was sure Chama was putting up a pretty good fight, holding eighty armed soldiers at bay, making a last stand with his back against the fence. Running out of ammunition was the only thing that would end the battle, unless the soldiers rushed the Comanche position in an all-out charge. With young inexperienced troops, it was not likely. Sam knew it would be a sad thing to watch, as the troopers gunned down Chama and the others, but Sam was determined to go. If he got there in time, maybe he could talk Chama into giving himself up before the soldiers killed him. It was an unlikely prospect, for Chama was sure to put up a fight until he ran out of bullets, but there was a chance he might listen to reason.

Long before he drove over a rise where a line of troopers stood behind a scattering of trees, Sam heard the occasional pop of a rifle above the noise of the motor. Below the trees a dry wash twisted along the newly strung barbed wires, marking the eastern edge of Kirk Ranch land. Sam stopped the car and walked to the group of soldiers; he found the young captain he had seen leaving the compound earlier in the day.

"How many?" Sam asked, looking past the trees toward the creekbank.

"We don't know," the captain replied anxiously, as a shot banged from somewhere to the left. "The way they hide themselves, I can't be sure."

Sam noticed the carcasses of two dead ponies near the fence. A closer look told him one of the ponies was a red and white paint, Chama's old stallion lying in a pool of blood. Sam felt a knot growing in his stomach. The Comanche escape had met a predictable end at the first wire fence.

"Tell your men to stop firing," Sam said, as he took his handkerchief from his pocket. "Let me try talking to them. Maybe they'll give up without a fight."

The captain gave the order to cease fire. Sam stepped around a tree trunk and waved the handkerchief over his head, hoping Chama would honor a flag of truce and allow him to come down to the creek for a talk.

Sam walked forward, trying to see any of the Comanche firing positions, hoping no stray bullets came flying from the creek before Chama saw his white flag.

"I want talk," Sam said in Comanche, as loudly as he could. "Do not kill me. We make talk first."

At first he could see no one in the dry wash. Then a head appeared above the rim, a face covered with black

56

mourning paint, bearing a red stripe from forehead to nose.

Sam lifted both hands to show he had no weapon, and stepped down the creekbank. What he saw made his hands fall to his sides.

Two old Comanche women glared at him. One was Pohawcut, the wife of Buffalo Hump, holding an old Navy Colt in her withered hands. The other woman, one he did not recognize, held a kitchen knife poised for a strike at Sam's belly.

"Why do you fight the soldiers?" Sam asked softly, wondering where Chama and the others might be.

"We follow Toyah Chama," Pohawcut said proudly. In spite of her age, the old woman was a fierce sight in black paint with the pistol in her hands.

"Has Chama gone to the west?" Sam asked, watching the gun shake in the old woman's hands.

Pohawcut looked away, keeping the truth in her spirit from the white man's eyes.

"I do not know. He is gone."

It was plain the two women were alone as Sam glanced around the creekbed. The soldiers had cornered two old women, and no warriors.

"I hope Chama makes it to Palo Duro," Sam said suddenly, as he looked into the frightened eyes of the women. It was the truth, in a strange way. Even though Chama had broken the law, Sam found himself hoping Chama might elude the soldiers.

"Poke has gone with them," the other woman said. "I wanted to be with my husband. We tried to follow, but the soldiers came and shot the ponies."

Pohawcut dropped the pistol near her feet, sighing.

"Only two bullets . . . not enough to fight so many blue coats. My grandson is with Chama. The boy is all I have left. My son was sent to the place called Florida. The boy's mother died giving birth. I will never see the boy again. There is nothing left for me but to die."

The two old women were a tragic sight. Apparently, the men left without them, knowing they faced a rough ride to stay in front of the soldiers.

"How many are with Chama?" Sam asked.

"Four," Pohawcut replied. "Poke, Conas, Quahip, and the boy John Yellow Bull. My grandson did not tell me he was leaving," she said, sobbing. "I followed their tracks to the canyon, then to the west. I brought Chama his fine war-horse, for the fight with the blue coats. They shot the pony. We could not find a hole in the white man's fence. We had no choice but to fight, with only two bullets."

The news proved Sam was right all along. Four old men and a boy were trying to ride west toward Texas. The Comanche revolt was a product of Tatum's imagination.

"Come back," Sam said softly. "There is no reason to die."

Pohawcut glared at him, lifting her chin.

"There is no reason to live, *Tosi Tivo*. Life on this reservation is worth nothing to a Comanche."

Sam picked up the pistol and took the knife, then led the women out of the dry wash toward the soldiers. He was sure a similar fate awaited Chama, perhaps even death, but he wondered how they had made it through the barbed wire fence beyond the creek. It looked like Chama had somehow found his way around the first of many fences in his path. Perhaps the old Sata Exiponi

58

were more cunning than he thought.

Two hours after the troopers left with the old women, Sam drove his car to a spot along the fence where four strands of wire lay on the ground, gleaming in the headlights of the automobile. Sam got out of the car and picked up one of the wires, examining the clean cut. Finally he turned west to look at the dark horizon, as a full moon lit the gently rolling hills.

"You old fox," he thought, grinning to himself. "You've learned a trick or two from the white man. I wonder where you found a pair of wire cutters?"

4

Their ponies splashed through the shallow water, following the course of the stream for half a mile before Chama swung west up the creekbank into the late day sun. There would be no tracks for the soldiers to follow, as the slow current swept all traces of the ten ponies' hooves from the streambed.

Poke dropped to the ground and cut a willow branch, sweeping the ponies' prints from the soft mud at the edge of the water, backing away to higher ground and a slab of limestone where the others waited.

Chama swept the eastern horizon, watching the skyline carefully for a dust sign. On the second day of their flight, there was still no sign of pursuit.

"The medicine of Quinne protects us," he said, feeling good after two days of freedom from the fort. "For many taums I have dreamed of riding a pony across our mother, the earth, without the eyes of the *Tosi Tivo* soldiers watching. We must ride hard to stay ahead, and be watchful for the *Tosi Tivo* farmers. This land has many more of the white man's villages than before. We must ride carefully."

He swung his pony away from the stream and followed a ravine angling roughly westward. Five times he had used the tool to cut through fences. By keeping to low ground, following dry washes and ravines, they avoided being spotted from the farms and settlements in their path. It was slow going—changing direction often to swing wide of a farmhouse—but necessary to keep from being seen. Chama knew how quickly the talking wires spread word among the *Tosi Tivo*. Time must be spent to hide their passage through the white men's farms, so no word would spread of a party of Indians.

For two nights they had ridden hard, changing ponies often to keep fresh mounts carrying the burden of a rider. During the day their progress was much slower, for they encountered many of the squat sod farmhouses. At a stream, Chama was forced to kill a barking dog with an arrow, before it warned a nearby farmhouse of their passing. Chama jumped down to retrieve the precious arrow, for their weapons were so few. If the soldiers came close, every bullet and arrow would be needed to keep the soldiers from running them down.

Single file, leading the spare ponies, they rode along a cutbank. Not a word was said among them, for the dry wind might carry the sound of voices a great distance. Chama was tired and hungry, and knew the rest were beginning to suffer from the ordeal. At the rate they were traveling—slowed by the need to stay out of sight during the day—the journey to Palo Duro would take five or six more days, without rest or sleep.

62

It would be a test of ponies and men, and the determination of the soldiers behind them.

But as he reined his pony around the cutbank, Chama felt better than he had in many taums, living the freedom he had dreamed of for so long.

Chama halted his pony suddenly. Beyond the cutbank he counted four fences stretching across their path, running north and south as far as the eye could see. Cattle grazed between the fences, some watering in a pool near a tower—like those Chama had seen at the fort—pumping water from beneath the ground. A wooden fan atop the tower squeaked with the movement of the wind, sitting on a bald prairie between the fences where eighteen taums before only empty land had been.

Four fences to cut through, on a flat prairie with no places to hide from the *Tosi Tivo*. It would be dangerous to ride out in the open to cut the wires, but with the soldiers somewhere behind them, Chama could not afford to wait for dark.

"I will go alone to cut the fence," Chama said, turning to the others. "Wait behind this hill, until you see me open the last fence. Then come quickly. If the *Tosi Tivo* come, swing back to the stream and wait. I will lead them north, then I will hide my tracks and come back to the stream."

Chama handed the rein of his spare pony to Quahip, then he took the tool and rode carefully to the first fence, sweeping the prairie with a close look before he dropped to the ground to cut the wires. The wire made a singing sound as the cutters broke the tension. He cut all four strands, then swung on his pony and hurried to the next fence, feeling the danger down the back of his neck.

Chama cut through the second fence and hurried to the third, galloping his pony, knowing it was foolish to ride openly through this treeless expanse in daylight. He knew this was not a brave thing to do, behaving like a stupid Kiowa, daring the *Tosi Tivo* to come for him. But so many fences left him no choice, for he knew in his heart that the soldiers were coming, and the time spent waiting for dark was too precious to waste.

At the last fence he saw three specks on the southern horizon, coming toward him along the wires. Three horses, trotting under a cloud of dust in his direction.

Chama hurried to cut the wires, then he swung on his pony and held his Spencer above his head, a silent signal to the other Comanches that the enemy was near.

Chama swung around to face the riders, knowing he had been seen, waiting for them to draw closer. It was his duty as Dog Soldier Chief to lead the enemy away from the main body of Comanches, risking his own safety so that the others could escape. Honoring this tradition would be expected of him, a Kwahadie warrior willing to give his life to save the rest of the band.

The riders drew near, three *Tosi Tivo* with their faces hidden under drooping hatbrims. Chama waited until they were very close before he lifted his rifle and let out a piercing war whoop, a challenge to any *Tosi Tivo* that would be understood by men who had fought Comanches.

Then Chama wheeled his pony and pounded his heels against the pony's sides, shaking the rifle at the white men as he gave another war cry and rode hard away from the fallen wires.

The men halted their horses and stared at Chama. Strangely, the *Tosi Tivo* stood and watched as Chama rode away. They did not follow, leaving Chama's challenge unanswered as they sat on their horses, talking among themselves. Chama wondered at first, as his pony ran easily beneath him, why the *Tosi Tivo* would not follow. Could it be the white men were cowards, or too stupid, like Kiowas, to understand his war challenge?

"I ain't been drunk fer two weeks," one rider said, blinking in the dust and heat, watching the horse and rider gallop away. "I know damn well I ain't seein' things, but that sure as hell looked like an Injun."

The oldest of the three squinted, shaking his head as the rider screamed at them again and shook a rifle in the air.

"That is an Injun, a mighty goddamn *old* Injun. I know'd this ol' ranch was pretty wild, but I never figgered to see no Injuns out here. What the hell you 'spose that old feller is doin' out here, cuttin' down all our new fence?"

"Stealin' cows, I reckon," another said, spitting tobacco juice in the dry earth as he watched the galloping horse move farther away. "I 'spect we caught him jest a'fore he stole some cows."

"Could be," the eldest said, wondering aloud. "I sure ain't lookin' forward to tellin' old man Higgins about his new fence. He's gonna be mad as a nest of hornets,

65

an' likely we'll be back out here in this heat, stretchin' new wire."

One of the cowboys scratched his chin and let out a long sigh.

"What worries me is what we're gonna tell Higgins 'bout this here fence. If we tell him an Injun was out here cuttin' down all this high-priced wire, he's liable to figger the three of us fer jakeleg drunks. Ain't nobody in his right mind gonna believe a story like that. If I hadn't seen that Injun myself, I wouldn't believe it either."

"What else kin we tell him?" the eldest asked, watching the Indian disappear over the horizon. "I ain't gonna tell Higgins *I* cut the goddamn fence."

"What do you figger one lousy Injun is doin' on this ranch all by hisself? That poor old horse of his was so scrawny, I'd be plumb ashamed to be seen ridin' it. From the looks of 'em, ain't neither one ate in quite a spell. Reckon the old feller was just plain hungry, lookin' fer a calf to kill?"

One rider shook his head.

"Hell of a thing to explain. I hope old man Higgins don't jest fire the bunch of us when we tell him the news."

They reined their horses around and started back to the south, keeping their mounts at a walk as they talked among themselves, deciding what they should do about the Indian. They were intent on a solution for their problem, and missed seeing four more Indians and nine ponies as they crossed the prairie behind them.

"I remember hearin' stories 'bout ol' Geronimo," the eldest said, probing his memory. "Now an' then

66

Geronimo would escape from some Injun reservation out west and go on the warpath again. Could be that was Geronimo we saw. He looked old enough to be Geronimo."

One rider spit in the dust and frowned.

"Good a guess as any, but I ain't lookin' forward to bein' the one who tells Higgins we seen Geronimo amongst his prize Hereford cows, cuttin' down all his brand new fence. Higgins will likely go on the warpath hisself, if that's what we claim we saw. He ain't gonna believe no Apache is out here on his ranch. My guess is, he's gonna fire the three of us, figgerin' we've got a bottle stashed at the windmill and earn the money he's been payin' us by gettin' wall-eyed drunk and seein' Injuns. That's what I figger will happen to us, if'n we don't come up with a better story."

The three rode in silence a moment longer, until one rider cleared his throat of trail dust and spoke softly.

"I need this job. Best we tell Higgins the truth, and hope fer the best. Besides, I can't dream up another story that'll fit all them busted wires."

They kicked their horses into a lope and rode to a sprawling ranch house outside Altus, Oklahoma. They tied their winded horses to a hitchrail with worried looks on their faces. All three went inside to give Edward Higgins the news about the Indian. When the story was finished they stood uneasily, puzzled by the look on Higgins's face as he walked to a table and picked up today's edition of the *Lawton Bugle*, remembering something, bits and pieces of a story on the front page he read just this morning. He donned his reading glasses and started a closer examination of the paper.

COMANCHES ON WARPATH AGAIN was spread across the front page, in bold headlines. Edward Higgins swallowed, and kept reading.

A band of Indian savages escaped the Fort Sill Reservation yesterday, according to Indian Agent Ike Tatum, chief administrator at the fort. As many as a hundred of the murderous Kwahadie Comanches, armed with rifles stolen from the fort armory, headed for parts unknown, have incredibly eluded cavalry patrols thus far. Lawton Sheriff Clive Davis has formed a posse to protect outlying ranches, but no one has sighted these savages and their whereabouts remains a mystery.

In a statement issued by Tatum yesterday, these Indians are described as armed and very danger- ous. Some have long criminal records with the Bureau of Indian Affairs, documenting the torture and scalping of hundreds of white settlers in Texas before their imprisonment at Fort Sill. One report indicates these killers may be headed for Texas. Texas authorities have been alerted to be on the lookout for mounted fiends dressed in warpaint and feathers. Over a hundred horses were stolen in the escape, indicating the force of Indians may be much larger than first suspected. Major Walter Townsend is directing military operations, as patrols sweep the countryside.

The reported leader of these Indians is a cold- blooded killer, a Chief named Toyah Chama, translating to "Scream of the Killer Pig."

Anyone sighting these red-skinned savages is urged to contact the Sheriff's Office at Lawton, or

Army Headquarters at Fort Sill. Tatum repeated his concerns that these men are some of the most dangerous criminals in America, and that citizens of western Oklahoma will not be safe until the Indians are captured and returned to prison cells.

Edward Higgins put down the paper and removed his glasses, thinking that one lone Indian could be a scout for the hundred escaped from Fort Sill. So many Indians could kill and feast on a dozen or more of his registered Herefords before they rode on toward Texas. He must send a wire to the fort at once, then notify the sheriff in Altus that a posse was needed, and quickly.

He left hurriedly for the telegraph office, knowing there was little time to waste before his prize cattle became a meal for the red-skinned fiends.

Sam Ault put aside his copy of the *Lawton Bugle* and shook his head. Most everything in the story was a distortion, aimed at focusing attention on Ike Tatum and his Comanche revolt. When the truth was finally known, Tatum would be a laughingstock. Four old men and a boy of fourteen had now become the object of a two-hundred-mile search by over four hundred cavalrymen, plus a posse from Lawton armed to the teeth with shotguns and rifles. A sad joke, but a joke that would probably cost Chama and his men their lives. Only when the bodies were counted would someone realize the horrible mistake. Inexperienced young soldiers and a mob of terrified farmers would shoot first, whipped into a frenzy by the story in the *Bugle*.

Four feeble old men and a child would die in a hail of misguided bullets, all because Ike Tatum wanted some publicity or public attention to break the monotony of his job on the reservation.

Someone should do something about this terrible hoax, he decided, as he came to his feet and stuck the newspaper under his arm. Someone had to try to prevent the tragedy before it was too late.

"I'm going to Tatum's office," he told Clara as he donned his hat from a peg near the door. "Won't be long, dear."

He drove rapidly toward the fort, deciding at the last minute that he would speak with Walter Townsend. The army could rectify the mistake easily. Call in the patrols, and let the Comanches alone until their horses played out. If Townsend notified the newspapers that this whole thing was a terrible mistake—that only four old men and a boy had escaped to ride peacefully toward Texas—the furor would die down and perhaps save the lives of the Indians. When the Comanche ponies broke down, it would be a simple matter to surround them and try for a peaceful ending. It made no sense to hunt them down with guns. The five would cause no trouble if they were left alone.

He knocked on Townsend's door as night fell on Fort Sill. Silently, Sam hoped his efforts were not too late, for with the full moon Chama would be an easy target for waiting guns.

Walter Townsend opened his door and gave Sam a grin.

"Come in, Sam. I was just finishing supper."

Sam took a seat in the small living room, admiring the military neatness of Townsend's quarters as the

70

major came from the kitchen with a bottle of whiskey and two glasses.

"Have a snort, Sam. Thins the blood."

He poured drinks and offered Sam a cigar, then lit his own and took a chair, puffing blue smoke toward his ceiling.

"What brings you, Sam? Any word about the Indians?"

Sam tossed his copy of the *Lawton Bugle* on a table.

"Have you read this, Walter?"

Townsend shook his head, then opened the paper to read the front page story as Sam sipped whiskey. Moments later Townsend dropped the paper in his lap, grinning.

"Typical newspaper, blowing up the facts. But why did you want me to read it?"

Sam put down his whiskey and leaned forward.

"Because it's bullshit, Walter. We both know this big Comanche uprising is only four old men and a boy of fourteen. With this story circulating all over Oklahoma, those Indians will be shot on sight by some half-crazy posse, or a green trooper who gets scared when he sees the first Indian. No sense in it. Why get these old men killed? Or the boy? All they're tryin' to do is ride to their old home in Texas. Tatum is tryin' to make a big name for himself out'a all this, maybe get a promotion. You can put a stop to it, Walter. Call off the troopers, and tell the newspapers the truth. Maybe nobody will get hurt, if you get the truth to the papers."

"It's out of my hands, Sam," Townsend replied. "Tatum is in charge of the Indians at Fort Sill. If he tells me to pick 'em up, or shoot them on sight, I've got to follow my orders. Same as bein' a U.S. Marshal, Sam.

71

Follow orders. I've got no choice."

"You could set the papers straight on how many Comanches you're lookin' for. It might help things die down a bit."

"Ain't my job. I told Tatum who was missing from the roll calls, but it's up to him to issue official statements from the Bureau. Besides, Sam, we aren't sure just how many are really missing yet. These redskins are sneaky. Some may have answered the roll call twice, to hide the fact some others are gone. I can't tell the bastards apart, Sam. They all look alike to me."

Sam sighed and leaned back in his chair.

"Then you won't help me straighten this out?"

Townsend shrugged.

"Ain't my job. What difference does it make to you in the first place? For Christ's sake, they're only Indians."

As Sam drove through the dark sighting the lights of his farm in the distance, he decided several things. Old age was a curse, not the reward he expected at the end of a productive lifetime. Were he a younger man—free of the debilitating pain in his joints—he would do something himself to help Chama. It was plain no one else intended to lift a finger to save the four old men and the boy. Tatum, and even Townsend, seemed to be enjoying their black comedy, perhaps thinking of the glory to be had in the newspaper accounts of the capture of renegade Comanches.

Also, were it not for the ache in his bones, he would have enjoyed swinging a fist into Ike Tatum's grinning mouth, when Sam asked him to stop the search for Chama, as if the request was preposterous. Townsend's reaction had been no different. In many ways it was a fate worse than death to be crippled and useless. If he were only a few years younger, with no pain in his joints, Sam would have enjoyed kicking the shit out of Ike Tatum and Walter Townsend. Their indifference to the plight of the Indians would have earned them every inch of Sam's boot leather.

5

A pony snorted, breaking the silence as the hooves of ten unshod ponies whispered through dry grass. A full moon bathed the rolling hills in silver light, as the Comanches rode west under a sky sprinkled with stars. A gentle breeze came from the west, carrying any sound, warning of the dangers ahead at a farmhouse or settlement. Chama led his spare pony at the front of the line to be first to hear any strange sound, first to see movement on the dark prairie in front of them.

All night, as he led the way across the treeless expanse, he thought about the Palo Duro, and the steep canyon walls of Pena Pah, where they would live for the remainder of their time on mother earth. These thoughts kept him from thinking about the hunger grumbling in his belly, and the sore muscles in his legs and arms after so many hours atop the pony. Quinne's medicine was strong enough to bring them one day's ride from *Nodema Pahehona,* the northern fork of the great river called "Red" by the *Tosi Tivo.* One more day's ride would bring them to *Pahehona* itself, the wide river marking the white man's boundary of Texas. By following *Pahehona*, they would come to the towering walls of the mouth of Palo Duro canyon. Chama could feel the presence of the canyon in his heart. It would be an end to eighteen taums of longing and dreams, when he rode into the mouth of Palo Duro again.

Suddenly, his pony gave a warning snort and halted, flaring its nostrils to catch a scent from somewhere ahead on the prairie. Chama could feel the pony's legs tremble, a warning that danger was near.

Then Chama saw the outlines of more than a dozen horsemen, moving across the moonlit hills, riding south across the path he must take to hold a westward direction.

"To-ho-baka," he whispered, the Comanche word for an enemy, warning the others to stay silent.

There was no place to hide the ponies, no low ground to wait for the passing of the distant riders. Another Indian would have easily spotted Chama in the moonlight, but the riders wore the *Tosi Tivo* hats of men who tended the cows.

Chama waited, motionless, feeling his heart pound with the danger of so many *Tosi Tivo* horsemen. Slowly the riders moved farther to the south, until Chama heard a distant cry in the white man's tongue.

"There they are . . . I see them!" a voice yelled above the wind.

Suddenly the horsemen turned and charged toward Chama, the sound of spurs rattling against their horses' sides as hooves beat along the dry prairie.

Chama whirled his pony and gave the signal to ride north as he kicked his pony into a run. The first gunshot boomed, echoing through the darkness as the ponies hit an all-out run away from the charging horsemen.

Poke answered with a bellowing shot from his Spencer, a sound that frightened the ponies into a harder run. Chama could see no fences in their path, and hoped the hills in front of them would hide none of the white man's farms as they raced over the dry grass ahead of the enemy.

Two more rapid shots came, then another, but the distance was too great for the bullets to find a mark. Chama let go of the rein of his spare pony and turned, bringing his Spencer to his shoulder, trying to find a target among the *Tosi Tivo*.

He picked a rider at the front of the pack and fired, feeling the jolt of the rifle slam against his shoulder. For eighteen taums the guns of Toyah Chama had been silent, keeping the treaty of Quannah. With his first shot came a flood of memories, of the many bullets he sent toward the blue coats in the battle at Palo Duro. The sound of his gun was a good sound, even with the danger of such a large force of white men charging after them. It was better to fight and die, if it was Powva's plan, than to wait in the stink of Fort Sill for death to creep up on him while he slept. It was better to die like a warrior.

For a mile the ponies held their ground, keeping a safe distance between them and the white men's horses. Gradually the *Tosi Tivo* fell farther behind, as the tough little mustangs kept a steady pace, pulling ground under their hooves without tiring.

At the top of a grassy knoll, Chama swung west, holding the direction they would need to reach Palo

Duro. Glancing behind, he saw the others riding easily on the backs of the running ponies, Taoyo first to follow over the rolling prairie. No more shots came from the distant shadows of the *Tosi Tivo;* their horses were winded by the long run.

Chama slowed his pony to a lope, reaching for the trailing jaw rein of his spare pony, while the wind whistled in his ears. After another half-mile, he pulled to a trot, glancing back, no longer able to see the group of white men on the plain behind them.

For better than an hour, Chama kept up a hard trot, putting as much distance as he could between his men and the pursuing riders. Crossing a ridge he selected a low spot and halted, letting the ponies blow while his men drank from their waterskins and chewed pieces of jerky.

After a brief rest, Chama pushed on until dawn. Without a word he dropped to the ground and changed ponies, then continued west into the purple shadows of dawn, stopping now and then to check their back trail. But the horizon was empty behind them. The ponies had outdistanced the *Tosi Tivo* horses. At least for the moment, their back trail was clear.

Chama fitted an arrow to his bow, and shot a rabbit as the ponies walked through clumps of tall prairie grass. Later, he killed another, then selected a spot under a thicket of brush to build a small fire and cook the rabbits.

Quahip skinned the rabbits quickly, then placed them on sharpened sticks to roast above the flames. Chama moved to the highest point above their camp to keep watch, smelling the delicious roasted meat while he scanned the skyline.

78

As soon as the meat was done, Taoyo took a portion and carried it to Chama. The boy's eyes begged to speak, but he held the silence like a warrior, while Chama ate the roasted rabbit. Without any training the boy was acting like a seasoned Dog Soldier, saying nothing as he followed the others. In spite of his few taums, Taoyo was no added burden on their journey, but rode his ponies with skill to match any of the others.

Finally, as Chama finished eating, the boy could stand the silence no longer.

"Have I done well, Toyah Chama?" he asked in a whisper.

Chama looked into his eyes, seeing no fear, even after the chase by the *Tosi Tivo* enemy.

"You will make a brave warrior, Taoyo. Your grandfather would be pleased."

The boy smiled and turned away to catch his ponies. Chama watched him with a touch of sadness, for the grandson of Buffalo Hump was a reminder of so many of the young Kwahadie warriors of long ago. In the days before the treaty, many young men like Taoyo had known the freedom of the plains. It saddened Chama that only one young warrior was at his side on their flight from the reservation. If only some of the others had come with them, the Comanches could fight the *Tosi Tivo* again in large numbers, winning battles, remaining free to roam the Staked Plains like before.

Poke quickly smothered the fire as Chama walked back to the ponies, to keep the smoke from leaving a telltale sign for the soldiers to follow.

As they made ready to leave their brief camp, Poke swung up on his pony and spoke to the others.

"We gave *To-ho-baka* a good fight. Our ponies are strong. We will see the Pena Pah again. It is good, to be free like in the days before the treaty."

Conas struggled up on his pony's back and grinned.

"The eagle sign was good medicine, Chama. For two days the air has smelled sweet, like clover in the spring. Lead us to the west, across the land of *Tosi Tivo*. We will fight them until all our bullets and arrows are gone. Lead us, great chief of the Sata Exiponi. Nothing can stand between us and the sweet waters of Pena Pah."

Quahip gave the yipping call of the coyote, throwing his head back to send his voice along the wind.

Chama sat his pony, hearing the joy in the voices of his old friends. Silently he thanked Powva, and the four great spirits, for delivering them from the reservation without harm.

He wheeled his pony and kicked into a trot, aiming due west as the others fell into a line behind him. In his heart Chama knew the journey was just begun, but for the moment he allowed himself a feeling of happiness, while his pony traveled easily under him.

An hour past dawn the land began to change. In the distance Chama could see a scattering of farmhouses and barns. The prairie became level, with square patches of plowed earth near the sod houses. As far as he could see in any direction, the land was broken by the *Tosi Tivo* plows. With the flattening of the land came another problem . . . there was no place to ride out of sight of the farms. Chama found himelf riding out in the open on a barren landscape that stretched to the horizon in every direction.

Chama halted his pony, and studied the plowed fields in front of him. Last night's encounter with the white men was proof that the talking wires had already spoken of Chama's escape. Parties of *Tosi Tivo* would be waiting for them wherever they rode.

Chama gazed to the south. An unknown distance away was the *Pahehona* and Texas. It would cost precious time to swing off course to ride toward Texas. But with so many of the *Tosi Tivo* farms in front of them, they had no real choice. It was better to avoid more fighting with the white men, with so few bullets and arrows.

He reined due south and kicked into a hard trot, hoping to get off the skyline as quickly as possible to avoid the eyes of the white farmers. Chama looked back and saw the worry in Quahip's eyes as he trotted close behind.

"I have never dreamed of so many *Tosi Tivo,*" Quahip said uneasily. "Like ants, they crawl over the land and build their lodges. We are so few, Chama. If they come, we must be ready to run the ponies hard, for there are so many we cannot win in battle."

Chama understood Quahip's concern. Even a brave warrior would not fight such overwhelming odds. It was better to leave no tracks and wait to fight another day, when the advantage was with his warriors. So few against so many was a foolish fight.

Far to the west Chama noticed a team of mules plowing the dry cornstalks. He swung east, pushing his tiring pony until he found a shallow depression where the ponies would not be seen by the farmer.

At midday they came to a fence. Chama cut the wires and changed ponies, then kept up the ground-covering trot to the south with his eyes westward on the scattered farms. Behind him the others held an uneasy silence, for they, too, watched the sod homes nervously, hoping no more of the *Tosi Tivo* horsemen came out to chase them.

Two more fences had to be cut as the afternoon wore away under a blazing sun. Chama hurried at each of the fences, feeling the danger down his neck, while he wondered if the white man's settlements would ever disappear from the land. Now and then, on distant roads to the west, they could see the progress of the wagons-with-no-horse, sending a plume of dust into the sky as they roared like angry cougars from one place to another.

As night grew close, Chama felt a growing concern about the direction they were taking. All the old landmarks were gone, the towering elms standing alone on the empty prairie, now uprooted by the farmers, were no longer there to guide Chama toward home. By riding so far south to avoid the farms, Chama found himself in a strange new land, crossing a flat prairie he had never ridden before. But still the farmhouses dotted the western horizon, so many that they seemed like a single village. There was no opening, no place where he could turn back to the west to ride in the right direction. And like Chama, the others wore their concern on their faces, especially the old Dog Soldiers who knew the trail to Palo Duro. Conas's face grew dark as he swept his eyes along the horizon. Like the rest, he knew it was a dangerous delay to ride so far to the south, but the clusters of sod houses gave no other choice.

At full dark Chama called a rest, dropping to the ground to rest his aching muscles. All five lay on the grass, exhausted by the hard day's ride, while the ponies grazed and gathered strength.

"Do you know the way?" Quahip asked softly as he lay beside Chama, speaking so the others would not hear.

Chama came up on his elbows, glancing at Taoyo before he replied.

"The big trees are plowed away by the *Tosi Tivo* and their digging machines. We are south of the old trail by many miles. The *Pahehona* lies somewhere to the south. If we have no choice, we will ride to the great river and cross into Texas, then follow *Pahehona* to the canyon. Many taums ago, this land was empty like we remember it. Now, there are so many *Tosi Tivo* we have no choice but to avoid a fight. Nothing must stop us from reaching Pena Pah, not the white farmers, or the soldiers. We must avoid a battle if we can, for our weapons are few."

Conas struggled to his feet, limping over to Chama as he glanced nervously over his shoulder.

"We must keep moving, Chama," he said in a whisper. "I can feel the hoofbeats of the soldiers in my heart. This is no place to rest . . . there is no cover, no places to hide. If the blue coats find us here, the fight will not last long."

They mounted fresh ponies and started at a walk through the darkness. In the distance they could hear the barking dogs of the farmers, and every now and then the roar of a horseless wagon. Chama and his men rode in silence, listening to the sounds carried by the night wind. For the first time since their escape, Chama began to worry about their hopes of reaching the Palo Duro. In all his dreams, he had never imagined there could be so many of the *Tosi Tivo* in the land that had

83

once belonged to the Comanches. Even the worst dreams of the peyote were not equal to this.

They stopped often to cut through fences, passing lighted farmhouses and the distant bark of the white men's dogs. No matter how far south they rode, Chama could find no opening through the clusters of *Tosi Tivo* farms that would permit them to ride west. Even in the dark, the sod houses were too close together. It would invite danger to ride so close to the farmers and their rifles.

As Chama stooped to cut another string of barbed wires, a strange sound reached his ears. Far in the distance thunder rumbled, yet he was puzzled by the thunder. The sky held no clouds, and the thunder was different in some way. It grew louder as Chama swung back on his pony. Then, to the north, he saw the light of a fire wagon . . . *Cona woba poke,* the white man's train.

He searched the dark prairie for the iron road that the train must follow. Two dark lines stretched across the grassy slope, only a quarter-mile from the fence where Chama sat his pony. The fire wagon would come very close, and there were no trees or low places to hide his men and the ponies.

Chama dropped to the ground.

"Stand behind the ponies," he said, moving quickly to the shoulder of his mount. "A fire wagon comes. Hold the rein tightly, for the sound of the fire wagon will scare them."

They held fast to the rawhide reins as the rumble of the train moved closer. The ponies danced and fidgeted, pulling away from the sound as the train roared down the rails in their direction.

The locomotive chugged past, so close that Chama could smell the smoke and see the fire from the boiler, as the ponies fought the hands that held them, snorting at the strange sight and bellowing sound rolling past. Chama counted nine cars, some with lights in the windows where people sat looking out at the darkness. If any of the *Tosi Tivo* saw the Indians, they would warn the driver of the fire wagon, and stop at the next village to send talk down the wires for the soldiers. Meeting the fire wagon was bad medicine, a sign sent by Powva that Chama must turn west to follow the flight of Quinne on a true course toward the canyon.

Chama waited until the fire wagon was out of sight, before he led his ponies through the fence to cross the tracks. Then he swung up and turned west, heeding the warning of the fire wagon to ride among the *Tosi Tivo* farms.

Soundlessly the unshod ponies walked through the plowed earth of a farmer's field, picking their way between dry corn stalks to travel between two of the sod houses. Chama fitted an arrow to his bow, knowing how great the danger would be so close to the farmer's guns.

A dog began barking, rushing toward them across the moonlit earth, struggling to run in the plowed ground. Chama drew back his bow and sent an arrow to silence the dog, knowing how quickly the angry bark would spread alarm among the *Tosi Tivo*. The dog yelped and fell silent. Then a door opened at the back of a sod house, and a lantern shed golden light on a farmer and the rifle in his hand.

"Who's out there?" a voice called. "What the hell's goin' on? Come here, Laddie."

Chama kicked his pony, bending low over the animal's neck as it broke into a run. He could hear the drumming hooves behind him as the others followed. For a time there was no sound from the farmer. Then a shot rang out.

Chama pulled the bow over his shoulder and lifted his rifle, turning back for a shot as another bullet whistled over his head, too high and wide of the mark. Chama kicked his pony harder, asking for a hard gallop, until the sod house was far behind them and the farmer's gun was out of range.

Chama slowed the pony, glancing at the dark prairie in front of him. Never had he seen so many of the sod houses. They had no choice but to run the ponies between them, hoping there would be no fences in their path.

It was the worst night Chama could remember, as he picked his way between the houses, swinging wide often to ride around fences, chased by the white man's dogs. It seemed the sod houses would last forever, stretching to the ends of mother earth. But at dawn they left most of the farms behind, entering broad flat fields of plowed ground, with only a handful of houses scattered widely on the horizon.

Suddenly, Chama heard the sound of a wagon-with-no-horse behind them. He turned quickly, when Poke gave the call of the owl, as the dust of the wagon appeared in a plowed field. He was surprised to see three of the horseless wagons bearing down on them, bouncing over the plowed earth as they sped in their direction. Chama could see many of the *Tosi Tivo* crowded in each wagon, and the gleam of rifle barrels in the morning sun.

Chama wheeled his pony and lifted the Spencer.

"They have come out to fight," he yelled, bringing the rifle to his shoulder. "Ride hard to the west. I will warn them with a bullet."

Poke raced his pony alongside Chama.

"I will stay. You must ride first, to use the tool if there are more fences."

Poke shouldered his rifle and fired at the first wagon, even though the distance was too great for any accuracy.

A volley of shots answered Poke's bullet, as the white men fired again and again from the jostling cars. Chama wheeled his pony and raced to the front, holding the course west over the plowed ground in a race ahead of the wagons. Chama glanced at Taoyo, finding him among the others, watching the boy ride easily on his galloping pony with no fear in his eyes. Taoyo showed the courage of his grandfather as the bullets sang over their heads.

Slowly the ponies pulled away from the *Tosi Tivo* wagons, and the shots died down to an occasional pop in the distance, until a stray bullet slammed into the ribs of Quahip's racing pony.

The bay staggered, trying to keep its footing as Quahip swayed on the pony's back. Before Chama could swing around to help Quahip, another pony raced alongside in a cloud of dust and a rider plucked Quahip from the back of his mount, just as the animal sprawled to the ground in a mass of flailing hooves and tangled legs. Taoyo pulled away just as the pony fell, with Quahip behind him. The boy had saved Quahip from being crushed by the falling pony. Even for a seasoned warrior, it was a brave thing, for the bay could easily have tripped a nearby pony in its fall.

Taoyo reined his gelding alongside one of the spare ponies, and while Chama watched, the boy grabbed the free rein and held it long enough for Quahip to make a flying leap to the back of the brown mare.

Then Taoyo looked at Chama, as a slow grin spread over his coppery face. They let the ponies run, leaving the wagons far behind, with Taoyo riding proudly among the rest, wearing a look that told of his test of courage.

They topped a gentle rise and Chama jerked his pony to a halt. A fence stretched across their path, touching the horizon in both directions. There was no way to ride around it. Chama would be forced to use the tool, and very quickly, with the farmer's wagons coming behind them.

He jumped to the ground and cut the top wire, but in his haste he dropped the tool. Before he could find it in the weeds near his feet, the sounds of the horseless wagons were very close. He cut the next wire, just as the first wagon came over the rise in a cloud of boiling dust. There was too little time to cut the other wires. They were trapped against the fence as the first gunshots rang out from the rifles in the wagon.

Suddenly, from the corner of his eye, Chama saw Taoyo galloping his pony straight for the uncut wires. In a brown blur the pony gathered its legs and jumped the remaining wires. As soon as the boy was clear, Conas kicked his pony and jumped the fence, leading his spare pony. Quahip followed. Chama swung on his pony and gave a fierce war whoop, sending his mount over the fence behind the others. Poke came charging toward the wires, and was soon behind the rest leading his spare mount. The *Tosi Tivo* guns boomed and echoed behind them, as they raced away from the fence. Chama turned back, watching as the first wagon came to a grinding stop at the uncut wire. The wagons could not jump the fence like a pony.

Some of the farmers jumped to the ground to fire their rifles, but the distance was too great for a moving target. Chama galloped to the front of the group and shook his rifle in the air, happy with their victory over the fence, and pleased with the courage of Taoyo. Buffalo Hump would be proud of his grandson. With a weapon, one day the boy would be a great warrior.

When the *Tosi Tivo* were no longer in sight, Chama slowed the ponies to a walk. To the west the land had begun to change again, becoming open grassland with a scattering of trees in the distance. They would find a place to rest the ponies, and to rest their aching muscles. The waterskins were low, and would need replenishing. If they could find a covering of trees, they might sleep for a few hours, changing guard to watch for the soldiers. Chama thought about the fire wagon, Powva's message that they must follow the flight of Quinne. It was good medicine, for the land was now empty in front of them. Once again, Chama dreamed of Palo Duro as the ponies walked through bunches of dry grass. With the blessing of Powva, Chama and his warriors would feel the deep grasses of Pena Pah again under their feet, and lie down to drink the cool water of the stream. In his heart he could feel the power of his spirit sign.

At midday they found themselves alone on a vast, rolling prairie dotted with stands of live oak. In their path Chama saw the deeper green of a willow tree, growing in a pocket deep within a forest of live oak. The willow told of a spring in the dry prairie, a place where they could water the ponies and fill their water-skins.

They rode into the trees, winding around thick tree trunks, until Chama found the willow growing at the edge of a tiny pool. They dismounted and watered the ponies, then hobbled them with their reins. Conas and Quahip fell to the ground, exhausted by so many days without sleep. Chama left the pool, walking to the edge of the live oak forest, and selected a spot where he could watch their backtrail for the soldiers. He lay down on a carpet of shaded grass, until he saw Taoyo walking through the shadows in his direction.

The boy knelt beside a tree, his eyes begging to speak.

Chama turned and handed the boy his rifle.

"Watch for the soldiers," Chama said softly, lying back on the soft grass to close his eyes. "You are a warrior now, Taoyo. You showed great courage at the fence. The lives of your Kwahadie brothers are in your hands. Keep a sharp watch."

The boy's face beamed with pride as he took the rifle. He turned to the east and scanned the horizon carefully before Chama drifted into sleep.

The slate-gray eyes of Quannah Parker rested on Sam until the story was finished. Quannah was tall for a Comanche, above six feet, with the pale eyes of his *Tosi Tivo* mother, Cynthia Parker. In Comanche, Quannah meant "stink," a name given to him at birth because all white people were believed to have a foul smell in the opinion of Comanches.

"My heart is heavy for Chama and my Kwahadie brothers," he said, speaking almost perfect English. "They will be killed before they reach Palo Duro. So much has changed. Chama could not know. He has been on the reservation for eighteen years."

Above Quannah's head, on a wall of the white man's house he owned in Cache, was a proclamation from the Governor of Texas, citing Quannah's efforts to end the Indian wars in Texas by signing the treaty. Sam read the framed document, signed by Governor Campbell, dated July 23, 1904.

"All they're trying to do is go back home," Sam sighed. "I thought you might know of some way to stop the army from killing them before it's too late. Only four old men and a boy. It seems a shame to have it end that way. They're harmless. Chama isn't looking for a fight. He just wants to go home to die in peace."

Quannah was silent, examining the *Tosi Tivo* marshal for a long time before he spoke.

"Some of my people are alive today, because I signed the paper with the white man. The soldiers shot down the women and children. We had no bullets . . . no food. I had no choice. I could not watch the soldiers kill them. But there are a few, like Toyah Chama, who would have fought Mackenzie until they died of a bullet. He would have chosen death in the canyon over life on the reservation. As War Chief, I made a choice for the children. Mackenzie promised food and blankets. I put down my guns forever. Chama is one of the old ones, and cannot travel the white man's road. He is already dead in spirit at Fort Sill. Perhaps it is better to let him live and die as he chooses. For some,

91

death is better than the reservation."

Sam got up slowly, thinking what a waste it had been to come for a talk with Quannah.

Quannah held up a hand, gazing out a window as he spoke again.

"I will talk with the soldier chief. I will ask him to let Chama and the others go to Texas. He will not hear my words in his heart, but I will ask him."

Sam walked out without giving a reply, doubting that any request from Quannah Parker would make a difference. Parker was a successful businessman in Cache, apart from his Comanche brethren in a clapboard house, removed from the blight of Fort Sill and the daily tragedy of Oklahoma Indians. A request from Parker to abandon the hunt for Chama would receive little notice at army headquarters. Tatum and Townsend would ignore it. The trip to Cache had been a waste.

Sam drove to his office on the main street of Cache, the U.S. Marshal's office for a ten-county area. Sam walked in and was greeted by Deputy Tom Ford, who was soon to be Sam's replacement and the youngest U.S. Marshal in the service. At twenty-nine Tom was young, but quite capable. It was Sam's recommendation that won Tom the job after Sam's retirement. Tom was a good peace officer, a wiry fellow with a keen sense of right and wrong. In many respects, Sam looked on him as the son he never had.

Tom stood up, grinning as he handed Sam a wire.

"This Comanche business has got everybody stirred up, Sam. Wait 'til you read this."

Sam scowled as he focused on the words.

"U.S. Marshal Sam D. Ault. Assist Department of

the Army with Comanche situation. Take all necessary measures to end revolt. Signed, Charles F. Peoples, Regional Office, Fort Smith, Arkansas."

Sam folded the wire and put it in his shirt pocket.

"Send a wire to Charlie that we'll do whatever we can. Might notify our Amarillo office that we think the Indians are headed their way. Be sure an' tell both offices that this revolt is only four old men and a boy."

Tom Ford let his jaw drop, fixing Sam with a look.

"It isn't a big war party? The paper said it was fifty or more."

Sam shook his head and made a sour face.

"Just four old men, so damn old and feeble they can barely sit a horse, and a kid of fourteen. Ike Tatum seems to think we need a little excitement around here, so he's blown everything up to make it sound like every Indian at Fort Sill ran off to scalp half of the farmers in Oklahoma."

"But have you read the *Lawton Bugle*, Sam?"

"I read it. It's all bullshit, Tom. I'm gonna drive out and have one last try at having Tatum set things straight. Be back later."

Sam stormed out of the office, then drove the twelve miles to Fort Sill with his mouth set in a grim line. He planned to set Ike Tatum straight on a few things, now that he had Charlie's telegram in his pocket, for it was Sam's official authorization to get involved. There would be a gray area as to who would be in charge of things, but Sam intended to try forcing Tatum to call off the soldiers. His plan would not work, if he knew Tatum at all, but it was worth a try anyway. Something should be done to stop a senseless killing of five harmless Indians.

Sam wheeled into Tatum's agency parking lot, noticing five dusty automobiles in the grassless yard.

"More reporters," he thought dully as he reached for the doorknob.

At the back, in Tatum's private office, Sam could hear the sounds of voices. As he walked in the room he recognized the woman from the *Lawton Bugle,* standing among a cluster of newsmen taking notes while Tatum talked.

Tatum looked up as Sam entered, a look of disappointment on his face.

"As I was telling these reporters, Sam, we have a wire from Altus reporting the sighting of our Indians. I thought the papers ought to know that the Indians are a good distance west of us. Maybe people around here can get some sleep now. The sheriff in Altus has a few of the facts a little mixed up, but I have no doubt someone saw our Comanches."

Tatum tossed a telegram in front of Sam. Sam picked up the wire and began reading.

"Commanding Officer, Fort Sill, Oklahoma. Two hundred Apaches from your Indian reservation sighted here at Edward Higgins Ranch. Leader identified as Geronimo. Send military assistance at once. Sheriff H.C. Tompkins, Altus, Oklahoma."

Sam shook his head in disbelief. Two hundred Apaches led by Geronimo. Since 1886 Geronimo had been in prison at St. Augustine, Florida. Chama had become Geronimo in the minds of frightened citizens, leading a force of two hundred Apaches.

Sam turned to the reporters and threw the wire on Tatum's desk.

"You can tell your readers this is all a mistake. This

94

Comanche revolt is only four old men in their sixties and seventies, and a child of fourteen. Five Indians, probably unarmed and certainly harmless, trying to ride back to their ancestral home in the Palo Duro canyon in Texas. This whole thing is a cock-and-bull story. Five Indians, too old or too young to harm anybody if folks will just leave them alone."

Tatum's face grew dark.

"We don't know how many there are, Sam. We haven't finished counting yet. We found the hoof-prints of fifty horses."

Sam turned to Ike Tatum, feeling his temper rise.

"I saw the tracks myself, Ike. Ten or eleven ponies. They took a few extra, since the army has starved their horses down to piles of skin and bones."

The reporters had stopped writing, looking from Sam to Ike Tatum. There was a tense silence, until Sam took the wire from Charlie Peoples and placed it on Tatum's desk.

"This is my official notification to get involved. You can tell Major Townsend I said to call off the troopers. I'm catching the train for Childress tonight. If I'm not too late, I'm gonna try to head off Chama before he gets to the canyon. I don't really expect them to make it that far, now that all this crap has been stirred up in the newspapers, but I intend to try. In the meantime, I suggest you wire the sheriff in Altus and tell him this is all a terrible mistake over four old men and a green kid."

Sam turned and glared at the reporters, a mean set to his chin.

"You're all at fault in this thing, writing all that crap without verifying the facts. I suggest you set your readers straight by printing the truth, for a change."

Sam stalked out of the office, slamming the door behind him.

Sam fired up the Star and drove away from the agency, thinking about the telegram from Altus. It was the telegram that finally pushed things too far, forcing him to take a hand in the search for Chama. All of western Oklahoma had gone crazy over Tatum's Indian uprising. Someone had to do something, at least make an effort to set things right before a mob of terrified farmers shredded Chama and the others with their guns.

6

Sam hurried through the front door, meeting Clara's surprised look as she dusted furniture in the living room.

"Pack my things, woman," he said gruffly, as he stomped over the hardwood floor toward the bedroom, still seething over the confrontation with Tatum and the reporters.

Clara placed her hands on her hips and stuck out her chin.

"You can speak to me in a civil tone, Samuel David Ault, and kindly tell me what you're in such a huff about. You may be a federal marshal, but in this house you have no jurisdiction. That badge doesn't mean a thing to me."

He stopped at the door leading to the bedroom, seeing the fire in Clara's eyes, and was at once sorry for the tone he used with her.

"Now, now, Clara dear. I'm in a hurry. Please pack my bags, and my saddlebags. This thing with the Indians has my backbone up. I'm sorry for the way I spoke to you. I'd rather face the entire Comanche nation on the warpath than have you in a temper at me. I'll be gone a week, maybe more. I've got to do something to help those old Comanches, before somebody shoots them. I've got to hurry to catch the late train for Childress. I'm taking Tom with me."

A twinkle came to Clara's eyes as she started for their bedroom.

"Shall I pack the salve from Dr. Roberts?" she asked, giving his cheek a loving pat as she walked past him to the closet. "Perhaps those youthful bones will need a rub, if you plan to spend much time on a horse."

He caught her arm and pulled her close, then he bent down and kissed her gently.

"I'll miss you, woman," he whispered. "I don't have any choice. I have to do something. I have to try."

Clara held him tightly, her face pressed against his chest.

"You old softie," she said. "Please be careful. You're not a kid anymore, Samuel. Don't let anything happen to you. I don't want to grow old all by myself sitting in my rocker."

He pulled her away and scowled.

"Don't make such a fuss, foolish woman. I can still ride a horse and take care of myself."

Clara nodded and turned for the closet, beginning with his saddlebags and slicker as she put clothes away for a ten-day ride.

Later, she fixed ham and biscuits in an oilskin, then kissed him as he hurried to pick up Tom Ford in time to meet the train.

He drove the Star as fast as he dared, never able to completely trust the steering wheel in his hands. With a pair of reins a man could steer a cold-jawed bronc in the right direction, provided the bit was severe enough, but the steering wheel gave him no such assurances. The Texas Southern left Lawton in less than an hour. With any luck he could catch the train and ride to Childress, then rent horses to ride across country to make a try at intercepting Chama along the Red River. His plan stood only a dim chance of success, for it was more likely that a posse, or a handful of worried farmers, would come across the hapless Indians first and gun them down.

Tom Ford asked no questions as he locked the office and got in the seat beside Sam. They drove to Tom's small house at the outskirts of Cache, while Sam yelled above the roar of the motor with an explanation for their quick departure. Tom ran inside, returning minutes later with his bags, waving to a pale, pregnant wife before they sped away toward Lawton.

As they drove, Sam explained their mission to his deputy, all the while thinking how glad he was to have Tom's company for the hot, miserable horseback ride that awaited them. Ford was a top lawman among the many Sam had known in a lifetime. He was a capable horseman, and a good man to have in a tight spot in spite of his short stature. In the eight years he had served as deputy, he had shown unusual dedication to the job. In three months, when Sam took his retirement, the marshal's job would be in good hands with Tom Ford.

At dusk Capt. Lloyd Braverman called a halt down the line of saddle-sore troopers and gave the order to dismount. Sergeant Hutto, a crusty old veteran from South Texas, barked the order and stepped down beside Braverman, shaking his head.

"Cap'n, we ain't never gonna ketch up at this rate. When a man's chasin' Injuns, he can't stop every time his ass gits sore."

Braverman turned, a look of scorn in his eyes as he looked down on the sun-blackened face of his sergeant.

"Have you ever fought Indians, Sergeant Hutto?"

Hutto looked away, wiping sweat from his brow.

"No sir. I ain't quite that old, Cap'n."

Braverman seemed satisfied as he turned to examine another freshly cut fence. Sixteen fences cut, by his count. He knelt to study the scattered tracks passing through the hole in the fence.

"Maybe forty or fifty horses," he thought. "With eighty mounted troopers, it'll be no contest."

Braverman straightened and looked west. Once they caught up with the Comanches, the battle would be short and sweet, a magnificent addition to his military record that would earn a promotion and a transfer from Fort Sill.

"Have the men see to their horses," he said sharply. "Ten minutes."

Hutto saluted, none too smartly in Braverman's opinion, then walked down the line of horses. Hutto was too typical of the army at Fort Sill, a misfit doing his time, living for discharge and a pension.

Braverman heard the sputtering of an automobile and turned as four carloads of men bounced over the prairie toward the resting troopers. From a distance Braverman could see the rifles and shotguns in every hand.

100

"Civilians," he thought wearily. "Local vigilantes. They'll only get in the way."

The four cars stopped near the front of the column. Armed men piled out, some dressed in overalls and flop hats. One had a star pinned to the vest of his suit, and a huge pistol tied at his waist. He eyed Braverman, then socked a Stetson over his thinning gray hair and walked briskly to the front of the column.

"Who's in charge here?" the man snapped in a tone that riled Braverman to the core. "Who's the commanding officer?"

"I'm in charge," Braverman sighed, "Capt. Lloyd Braverman."

The man gave Braverman a quick look of appraisal as he stuck out a hand.

"I'm Sheriff Nelson Dobbs, from Mangum. These men are my deputies. We got a wire 'bout these damn Apaches, and come quick as we could to head 'em off. Have you found any tracks?"

Braverman pointed toward the hole in the fence.

"Maybe forty or fifty unshod horses. The tracks are pretty fresh."

Sheriff Dobbs glanced at the hoofprints.

"Don't look like so many to me," Dobbs replied thoughtfully.

"This is army business, Mr. Dobbs. We'll handle it."

Dobbs turned and clamped his jaw.

"Like hell it is, son. Any time a bunch of murderin' Injuns rides through my jurisdiction, it becomes my goddamn business. I don't want no quarrel with the army, but I'm the lawful sheriff in these parts, and I aim to see them Apaches don't raise no hell around here."

Braverman shook his head, glancing at the posse.

101

"First of all, the Indians are Comanches. Second, they escaped from a military reservation. This is an army affair, Mr. Dobbs. I suggest you stay out of our way, because somebody might get hurt. These Comanches are armed and dangerous."

Dobbs stepped a little closer to Captain Braverman, a mean look in his eyes.

"Listen to me, sonny. I was carryin' a gun before you was born. I'm the sheriff in this county, and I'll do as I damn well please. Personally, I don't give a damn if they're Kickapoos, when they come around Mangum, they'll have to contend with me. I hope I made myself real clear, 'cause I aim to stay after Geronimo and his bunch 'til they cross the Red River."

Braverman threw up his hands and turned for his horse.

"Suit yourself, Mr. Dobbs. By the way, Geronimo isn't with them. He's an Apache."

Sheriff Dobbs stood his ground while Braverman mounted.

"I don't care who they are," Dobbs said again, "they ain't gonna lift no scalps around here."

Hutto gave the order to ride, and the column moved forward through the hole in the fence into the deepening twilight. The posse from Mangum climbed back in their cars and roared through the fallen wires behind the soldiers, until Sheriff Dobbs barked an order and the cars raced around the trotting cavalry horses to be first behind the Indians, obliterating most of the hoofprints with tire tracks as they roared into the night ahead of the soldiers.

*   *   *

Chama rode his pony to the edge of the water and sat in the deep shadows of a cottonwood tree. *Nodemah Pahehona* stretched in front of him, the north fork of the great river that would lead him to Palo Duro. Chama waited in the darkness, listening for several minutes to the night sounds, the chirping of crickets and the calls of night birds from the far side of the river. If there was no danger, there would be no disturbance in the usual sounds that came with the dark. It was one of the earliest lessons taught to Comanche children, to heed the regular heartbeat of mother earth. If something was wrong, if danger lurked close by, a listening ear would notice the disturbance, or the strange silence of mother earth's creatures when something unusual moved through the darkness.

Chama knew it would be a tricky crossing, in spite of the dry summer. The river ran deep and wide. The Comanches knew a traditional crossing somewhere to the north, marked by a flat butte. Because of the many *Tosi Tivo* farms, Chama was far south of the crossing.

Poke moved his pony beside Chama's, gazing worriedly at the current.

"The water is deep, Chama. Our ponies are tired from the hard ride. *Nodemah Pahehona* will try to claim a sacrifice in the deep places. We must find a shallow crossing."

Chama glanced over his shoulder at the dark horizon.

"There is no time. All day the *Tosi Tivo* chased us in their wagons. They will be close. We must ask Powva for strong medicine and cross the river here."

"It is dangerous, Chama. The ponies are tired."

Chama lifted both arms to the sky and began a soft

103

chant, a prayer asking for a safe crossing of the river. One by one, the others joined Chama, repeating the words almost forgotten after eighteen taums.

Chama lifted his rein and nudged his pony into the shallows. The rest followed silently, knowing a tired pony could cost them their lives in the moonlit river.

Chama had ridden only a few yards when he felt the current lift his pony off its feet. He slid from the pony's back and let go of the rein, twisting his hand in the pony's mane to float alongside the swimming animal. He turned to watch as the boy slipped off his pony's back, releasing his jaw rein like the rest. If a pony had its mouth pulled open while swimming, it would drown very quickly. Taoyo had been taught the lesson. He had known to let go of the rein.

The cool water felt good on Chama's skin as the pony struggled through the current, its hooves thrashing to keep its head above the surface. Behind him Chama could hear the weakened ponies gasping for breath as they fought the current, puffing like the white man's train as they swam toward the far bank. Chama thought of Conas, his old hands weakened by the sickness in his joints, and hoped that Conas had the strength to hold on to his pony's mane long enough to reach the other side. In the moonlight Chama could not find Conas among the swimming ponies and bobbing heads of his warriors. Chanting softly, Chama prayed for Conas's safety in the river.

Suddenly, Chama heard the sickening sound of a strangling pony, frantic coughing to rid its lungs of water, then the splash of a mighty struggle to stay above the surface.

Chama turned, just as Taoyo gave a soft cry. The

boy's pony went out of sight below the silvery water, churning white foam.

Taoyo splashed noisily, flailing his arms about in a desperate attempt to stay afloat. Like all Comanches, the boy did not know how to swim, believing it was nature's intent that only animals were meant to wade deeper than they could stand.

There was nothing Chama could do to save the boy. He could not turn his swimming pony, for a pull on the rein would drown it as quickly as Taoyo's. He could do nothing but watch, gripped by a terrible sorrow while the boy drowned, unable to keep his promise to Buffalo Hump. In spite of their prayers, the river would claim a life.

Then Chama saw a head bobbing along the surface beside Taoyo. A hand came out of the water, grabbing the boy's hair. Chama looked closely, recognizing Conas as the old man pulled Taoyo above the water. Conas had let go of his pony's mane to try to save the boy, a very brave thing, since like the rest, Conas could not swim.

Yet somehow, Conas and the boy were being pulled through the water. At first, Chama could not understand how Conas was able to swim in the strong current, holding the boy's hair with one hand to keep his face above the surface. Then, as Chama looked closer, he understood. Conas was holding on to the tail of one of the swimming ponies, and was being pulled through the inky water toward the safety of the bank. Conas had grabbed his pony's tail and rescued Taoyo. It was an answer to their prayers. Powva had given Conas the strength to hold on to the tail while he held Taoyo and kept him from drowning. It was an act of courage, as brave a feat as any Conas had shown in battle. The murky river was just as dangerous as any enemy, yet Conas had defeated the hands of death at the bottom of *Nodemah Pahehona.*

Chama's pony found its footing, struggling through the deep mud to the river bank, then shaking the water from its coat as Chama knelt in the shallows, exhausted. The other ponies splashed out of the river, gasping for air as the five men sank to the mud beside Chama.

Conas and Taoyo came last, walking together to the grassy bank before they fell to the ground, gasping like the ponies.

"I cried out," Taoyo said, choking water from his lungs. "I was afraid of death. I am sorry."

Chama stood up wearily and walked over to Conas and the boy. He looked at Conas, then gave the sign of a brave heart in battle. Then he looked down at Taoyo, speaking softly.

"Even a brave warrior must fear a thing he does not know how to fight. All men are without power in a river. It is the way of mother earth since the beginning of time. With the power of Powva, Conas kept you from the hand of death. It was Powva's plan that your life was spared. Say the prayers of thanks to the great spirit, and say no more about your fear."

Taoyo turned to Conas, his eyes filled with the words he wanted to say. Conas placed a hand on the boy's shoulder.

"Help me to my feet," Conas said, grinning. "We must ride hard to put distance between us and the *Tosi Tivo.*"

They caught their ponies and rode away from the

106

river, five tired men and nine worn ponies pushing westward into the night. All night Chama kept up a steady pace, changing ponies more often as the animals suffered after so long without grain and rest.

At dawn Chama fitted an arrow to his bow and killed a doe, resting beneath a thicket of elm branches in a dry wash. Poke dropped off his pony and began skinning a hindquarter. Chama rode to a knoll and kept a watch while Quahip and Conas built a small fire. It was good luck, finding the deer, for their food was gone and all needed a rest. Taoyo hobbled the ponies in deep grass, giving them badly needed nourishment and rest.

Chama worried about the delay, but found the horizon clear in every direction. The elm grove hid the men and ponies well enough to chance the brief rest stop.

Chama rode down to the fire and hobbled his pony, smelling the roasting meat as the smoke from the tiny fire filtered up through the elm branches. Poke cooked the hindquarter while the others rested, lying in the shade to catch a few minutes of badly needed sleep.

They feasted on deer meat and sipped water from their skins, while the ponies grazed hungrily on the dry grass.

"One more day and we come to the big river," Conas said around a mouthful of venison. "The farmers' houses are gone. We must be very close, Chama. This land is empty, like we remember it. The canyon will not be far."

"Maybe three more suns," Chama replied, gazing west. "The ground begins to turn a red color. We are close to *Pahehona*. If no more of the *Tosi Tivo* come to chase us, the ponies will be strong enough to make

107

it to Pena Pah."

Quahip looked back to the east, worry on his face.

"So many of the white men came after us. I did not know there could be so many. In my dream back at the fort, they were like a robe covering the earth, but still I did not dream of such a great number. They will be coming, Chama. We must hurry to reach Palo Duro. In the canyons leaving the river, we will have places to hide. Out here, they can find us easily."

Chama came to his feet, licking the last of the roasted meat from his fingers.

"They will come. But we will be ready. The ride is hard, but it is better than sitting in the stink of the fort. I can smell the sweet air, and the eyes of the *Tosi Tivo* soldiers are not watching us. We are free, like the promise in Quinne's sign. I will fight the soldiers wherever they find us, but I will not go back to the reservation. I will drive my *Ma-wea* in the ground, and fight until a bullet stops my heart. No words in a treaty paper will make me put down my rifle again. I choose death rather than a single day as a prisoner of the *Tosi Tivo*."

The others agreed quickly with a sign. Conas struggled up on his swollen joints and shook a fist in the air.

"I will kill many of the blue coats if they come for us. For these few days, even with the pain in my bones, have been happy, like in the days of our past. Let them come! I will die fighting them beside Chama."

Poke tied the remaining meat on his pony, then they broke camp and rode into the afternoon heat, keeping their ponies at a steady walk across the empty prairie toward *Pahehona*. All of them kept a keen eye on the eastern horizon, turning back often to study the sky.

108

line, certain that the soldiers were coming along the tracks of the ponies.

Sam climbed down from the train, stiff after so long in the hard seat and sick to his stomach from the smoke blowing past the open window. Young Tom Ford looked fit enough, testimony that old age made any journey more difficult, even in the relative comfort of a train.

"I'll get our baggage, Tom," he said with a sigh. "You walk to the livery and find us two good horses. Tell 'em we'll need them for a week or better. When they see your badge, likely they'll pick two good trail horses. Everybody ought'a know Fort Smith don't pay to rent lame horses."

Tom walked down the loading platform toward the streets of Childress as dawn broke to the east. Sam retrieved their baggage from the platform and carried it to a hitchrail at one end of the depot.

"Hell of a thing," he muttered to himself, as he sat on a bench to wait for Tom. "When a man gets so damn old his knees won't work, he ought'a just lay down and starve himself to death. Legs ain't worth anything without good knees."

A grubby child of eight or nine, too long without a bath, came down the platform selling the latest edition of the Childress newspaper. Sam bought a copy, wondering if the story of the runaway Comanches had reached this part of Texas.

He opened the paper, shaking his head as he read the big headline spread across the front page.

"INDIAN ATTACK POSSIBLE FOR CHIL-

DRESS" was printed in bold type at the top of the paper. Sam sighed and read further.

A warlike band of savage Comanche Indians fought their way free of the Fort Sill Indian Reservation in Oklahoma, and may be headed for the Texas panhandle, according to army sources at the fort. Major Walter H. Townsend is quoted as warning citizens of the panhandle region to be prepared for a possible Indian attack by a big party of armed Comanches, under the leadership of a famous chief named "Screaming Killer of White Pigs." Horseback divisions are in hot pursuit, following these bloodthirsty killers toward Texas.

Although it has been almost twenty years since the last of the American Indians surrendered, this renegade band is listed as a group of hardened killers with a history of scalping white people and murdering women and children. Townsend urges residents of the Texas panhandle to take every precaution until they are caught.

Sam did not finish the story. He dropped the paper in his lap, wondering where Chama might be at this moment. With all this frenzy stirred up in the papers, it would be a miracle if he and the others were still alive. Every gun in the area would be loaded and ready for the sighting of an Indian. In all probability, Sam and Tom were too late to do anything to help them.

Yet, in spite of the overwhelming odds against them, Chama had somehow made it through the heavily populated country beyond Altus. A simple pair of wire

110

cutters enabled him to hold a westerly course for over a hundred miles to Higgins Ranch. By some miracle, the Comanches had eluded swarming posses and soldiers, staying far enough out in front to avoid a major confrontation for at least three days and nights. It did not seem possible, knowing the country Chama had come through, but apparently the old Indians and the boy possessed more cunning than Sam thought. In spite of his age, Chama was still a fast-moving shadow, like the warrior he had been when he roamed the Staked Plains two decades ago.

Tom came riding to the hitchrail on a long-backed black gelding, leading a saddled buckskin with broad, flat cannon bones. Both horses looked to be good for a long day's ride, if a man could judge by the looks of them. After a couple of hours on the trail, the truth would be known.

They tied their gear behind the high-backed saddles. Sam had not brought a gun, but Tom wore a gunbelt with a .44 Colt, and a small-bore rifle to hunt wild game. Sam was sure no guns would be needed with Chama, if they found him at all along the river below the canyon mouth. Talking would be the only way to bring Chama back, a slim hope, knowing how much Chama hated the reservation in the first place. If it came down to guns, Sam knew he could never bring himself to take a shot at Chama. He would not, no matter what, carry the death of the old Indians and the boy on his conscience.

Sam lifted one foot and climbed painfully into the saddle. It had been a year or more since he last rode a horse, for the pain of a day in the saddle had convinced him that the seat of the Star touring car was something he must resign himself to for the rest of his days. The Star had been a gift from Charlie Peoples for Sam's last year as marshal for the district, a way of keeping Sam on his rounds over the ten-county area until his retirement.

Sam reined the dun away from the rail and kicked into a trot, feeling sharp stabs of pain through his legs as he and Tom rode through the silent streets of Childress. A warm morning sun came at their backs, as the two men left the city onto a rolling prairie dotted with live oak and elm. A sudden gust of wind sent dust devils swirling around them, whistling as they blew past.

"How far is Palo Duro canyon?" Tom asked above the wind, glancing at the pair of canteens he had filled at the livery. "I hope we have enough water. It sure looks dry out there."

"Maybe three days," Sam replied, pulling his hat low over his face to keep the dust from his eyes. "Rough country. Damn little water, except for the river. Been a long time since I rode this range. I'd guess three days, maybe more."

Sam watched the horizon, feeling the heat build on the open grassland. It would be a long, hot ride to the mouth of the Palo Duro, unless they crossed Chama's trail along the river. With the dry year, tracks would be hard to find, if he could find them at all, for there was nothing on earth any harder to track than a mounted Comanche.

They left Childress behind, alone on the road to Amarillo at this early hour. The buckskin traveled easily, a soft trot that was kind to Sam's arthritis, covering ground with each long stride. For the moment, at least, Sam felt good in the saddle again. Riding a horse through the open spaces was a joy, without the sharp pains in his legs. Tom Ford would never know the peace of the open rangeland, for an automobile and telegraph lines were doing the job that was once only possible on the back of a horse. A mounted peace officer's time was past, like the covered wagon. Things were changing rapidly before Sam's eyes, and in truth he did not like them.

They rode in an easy silence for several miles, enjoying the quiet with only the sounds of shod hooves clicking over rocks in the road. They passed a few wagons, bound for Amarillo and Sante Fe, but for the most part, the road was empty of travelers. Now and then an automobile roared past toward Childress, spilling dust over everything in its path. Sam cursed them silently, knowing his Star left the same choking cloud of dust in its wake.

They followed the road for a pair of hours, until Sam saw a distant green line marking the winding course of the Red River.

"Best we swing north," he said above the wind. "I figure Chama will keep the river in sight as he makes his way west. With the country changed so much, he'll need a landmark he can recognize."

They trotted to the south bank of the river before Sam swung west. The ground was bright red, a clay the color of blood that would reveal a hoofprint to the careful eye. They passed herds of grazing cattle along the river, but they saw no ranch houses or farms as they pushed farther west under a boiling sun.

Sam studied each stretch of barren ground carefully as they rode. Deep in his gut he knew it was too soon to encounter the tracks of the Indians, even if Chama's cunning enabled him to pass through the thickly populated country north of the river. It was an old habit, to study the ground wherever he rode, looking for the smallest detail, for they often led to the most important discoveries. It was a part of his job as a peace officer. Even the most careful men made an occasional mistake, leaving a telltale sign of their passing. Keen eyes and infinite patience led to most of the break-throughs in tracking another man.

By mid-afternoon Sam felt hungry and called a halt to rest the horses in a grove of live oaks beside the river. Sam opened his bedroll and handed Tom a pair of biscuits, each with a slice of ham inside that reminded Sam of Clara's home cooking.

Tom gazed thoughtfully across the river as he chewed his lunch, watching a pair of buzzards flying in lazy circles.

"Have you figured out what we're gonna do if we find these Comanches?" he asked idly.

Sam shrugged, wondering just how he *would* handle things if they found Chama.

"Try an' talk 'em into going back, I suppose. I've thought about it some. Chama ain't likely to just give himself up. If they're armed, I 'spect they'll put up a fight."

"Are we gonna shoot back if they take shots at us?"

Sam sighed, blinking as he looked across the river.

"Damned if I know, Tom. They've broken the law by leaving the reservation. It's our job to bring 'em in if we can. To tell the truth, it don't make sense to make all this fuss over these few Indians, but I can see the army's view. If they let these five go, what's to keep the others

114

from runnin' off? If it was up to me, I'd just let 'em be, at least for a little while. In a few months, a patrol could ride in the canyon and track them down. At least they'd have been free for a little while."

Tom sipped water from a canteen, then he stood up and dusted off the seat of his pants.

"Unless I missed it, I don't think you answered my question. What'll we do if we find them, and they won't come back peacefully?"

Sam got up and pulled his hat low over his face.

"Damned if I know, Tom. It ain't likely Chama can make it this far, but if he does, I guess we'll have to cross that bridge when we come to it. Hell of a thing for me to explain, but I came out here to try saving their lives from a posse and the soldiers. I don't think I could shoot ol' Chama if it came right down to it, even if he took a shot at me first. Like I said, I can't explain things proper, but I had to try something. I couldn't just sit at home and let somebody kill the old Indians for wantin' to be free again. That's all they want, just to be left alone out in the open spaces. They don't mean any harm."

"Damn shame," Tom said as he walked to his horse. "Seems like a big waste of everybody's time, having so many folks chasin' a few old Indians. When I read the Lawton paper, I figured we were in for one hell of a fight, trying to capture so many of them. If folks knew it was only four old men and a kid . . ."

"We have Ike Tatum to thank for all the fuss," Sam said, as he pulled himself into the saddle. "Still, Chama has broken the law. I suppose that's what I'm doin' out here, tryin' to enforce the law. For better than forty years, I've made my livin' seein' to it that folks obey the

115

laws. I've done it so long, I don't reckon I could change, even if I wanted to. Old habits are hard to break. A man has to do what he knows is right, even if it don't suit him every time. I ain't gonna be 'specially proud of myself if I have to arrest four half-dead Indians and a kid, but it's my job, like it or not. Yours, too. Best we get on with it."

They rode out on the prairie at a trot, crossing a plain thick with wild grasses and dotted with clumps of live oak and elm. Sam studied the ground, certain there would be no tracks, but following old habits just the same.

At dusk they picked a campsite in a grove of trees along the river. Tom built a fire and started coffee, then unsaddled and hobbled their horses. Sam stretched out on his saddle blankets to rub some of the salve on his aching knees.

"It's hell to turn old, Tom," he said, wrinkling his nose at the smell of camphor. "I can't remember just when it hit me that I was gettin' too old for most things. Seems like, all of a sudden, I couldn't get around like I used to. First I cussed and fussed about it, making all sorts of excuses about the weather and bein' tired. Then it came to me I was just plain old. Damnedest thing I ever faced, Tom. When it comes your turn, it won't be much different. Just accept the black truth that you're done-in, like an old plow horse with a big fistula on its withers. Times I wish I could just go off some place and slit my own throat to be done with it. I can't do it, of course, but it would put an end to all this feelin' sorry for myself over bad knees."

Tom grinned, knowing Sam was only feeling the urge to complain.

"Clara says it's a waste of time trying to argue with you about old age. She told me the only thing wrong with your joints is all that hardheadedness run down to your knees."

"Women," Sam grumbled, tossing the salve to one side. "When Clara and I were both young pups, she held her mouth shut and done what I told her. Lately, all that woman knows to do is flap her gums together at me, like she knows all there is to know on any subject. Time comes in a man's life when he needs a little peace and quiet, and all he gets is empty-headed talk from a woman. Ought to be a law against women opening their mouths, unless some fool asked 'em to."

Tom chuckled. It was not his first time listening to Sam's opinions on the subject of women. Tom knew how much Sam loved Clara, but when Sam's joints were bothering him, he took a swipe at anything in sight, including his devoted wife. There was nothing to do except let Sam gripe, until he vented all his anger over his ailing joints.

They ate ham and biscuits, sipping scalding coffee under a star-filled sky. Finally Sam lay back against his saddle and fell asleep. Tom sat by the fire, thinking about the five runaway Comanches, wondering what Sam Ault would do if it came down to a confrontation with Chama. There was an odd difference in Sam's voice when he talked about Chama, an uncertainty Tom had never heard before in the eight years they had been together as peace officers.

He counted nine horses in the half-light of the moon, nine horses walking through the trees at the edge of the cotton field. He gripped his rifle with sweaty hands, listening to the soft sounds of hooves moving toward him.

Caleb turned to his brother and whispered a warning.

"You was right, Bobby Joe. Here they come. Look over there, in them trees. I counted nine. Let's make sure we can see 'em real good before we start shootin'."

Behind a rotted tree trunk five men waited, rifles and shotguns aimed at the corner of a cotton field surrounded by barbed wire. Caleb Sikes and his brother had talked all day about what they would do with the one-hundred-dollar reward, posted for the head of even one of the murdering Apaches. It had taken the Town Council of Dodson, Texas, only one hour to raise the reward money from area businessmen and ranchers. One hundred dollars to the man who killed the first Apache who tried to raid a Dodson farm or break into a store to steal more guns. Word of the Apaches had come in a telegram from Altus, Oklahoma, a warning to Dodson Constable Seth Meeks to be on the lookout for renegade Apaches led by Geronimo.

Caleb Sikes knew the lay of the land around Dodson. There was a shallow crossing of the Red River below his cotton field, a perfect place for the Apaches to lose their tracks. Caleb gathered three cousins and hurried to the cotton field before dark, to set a trap for Geronimo and his men.

Efram Sims cocked his 30/30 and sighted along the barrel, waiting for an Apache to appear in his sights. A hundred dollars was a huge sum, enough to take the worry out of farming next year. He knew he was a better shot than any of his cousins, even Caleb. Efram could feel the hundred-dollar bill in his hands, as he drew a bead on the first shadowy figure beside the fence.

A horse stepped out of the trees into the moonlight. Efram could wait no longer. Only one Apache was needed to claim the reward.

He squeezed the trigger and felt the rifle slam against his shoulder, as the explosion ripped through the silence.

A horse screamed in pain. Efram saw a shadow tumble to the ground as the eerie cry of the wounded animal filled his ears.

Four more guns exploded at once, flame belching from the barrels as a wall of noise roared through the clearing. Beyond the fence the trees were filled with moving shadows, as Apaches swarmed toward the rotten tree. Five rifles fired again and again, sending a barrage of shells toward the swirling Apaches. Another horse whickered in pain as bullets knocked it to the moonlit ground.

Efram levered six shells at the Indians, firing as rapidly as he could, trying to find a target in the billowing gunsmoke. Bobby Joe's shotgun roared above the sounds of the rifles. The wounded horse struggled to rise at the edge of the field, legs thrashing as it coughed and whinnied with fright and pain. Someone fired again, sending a bullet into the horse's chest that sent it crashing on its side.

"It's a goddamn horse!" Caleb yelled angrily. "Shoot the goddamn Indians, you idiot."

Gradually the gunfire died in silence. The five waited, searching the dark trees for a target. Somehow,

119

all the Apaches had disappeared. Nothing moved in the forest, and there was no sound.

"They'll be comin' around behind us," Efram stammered, thinking of what it would be like to have two hundred Apaches creeping up on them from the trees. "Let's get the hell out'a here. We can come back at sunup to get the ones we killed."

Caleb and Bobby Joe turned, crouching beside the tree to examine the area behind them.

"Let's git," Caleb whispered. "I know I shot the first one we saw. I had a clean shot. I saw him fall off his horse."

Caleb received little argument from the others as they crept away from the tree, for they were too busy watching the shadows for the first wave of Apaches coming to overrun their position. One dead Apache was all they needed, and Caleb shot him right off his horse with his first shell. They all saw it clearly, for the dumb Indian had ridden right out in plain sight.

Chama slowed his galloping pony, looking for the others in the deep shadows of the forest. He reined to a halt in a ravine and waited, listening for the running hooves of his warriors' ponies.

One by one the others galloped into the ravine. Chama counted four riders and only five ponies. Chama's pony was killed by the first bullet. Before it fell, he jumped to the back of his spare mount, just as the gunfire erupted from the dead tree across the field. His eyes and ears had given Chama no warning of the ambush. The fault was his that the *Tosi Tivo* guns had taken them by surprise.

Quahip rode up beside Chama. Suddenly, Quahip slumped over his pony's neck. A soft night wind brought Chama the scent of blood.

Chama jumped to the ground and grabbed Quahip as he slid from the animal's back.

"It is bad, Chama," Quahip gurgled around the blood in his mouth, as Chama lowered him to the ground.

A dark stain was spreading down Quahip's chest. Chama found the ragged edges of a bullet hole in Quahip's neck, just below his left ear. Blood pumped in regular bursts from the ugly wound, covering Chama as he held his old friend in his arms on the moonlit grass.

Softly, Quahip began singing his *Nie habbe weichket,* the death song gurgling in his throat as blood entered his torn windpipe.

One by one the others dismounted, coming to stand over the dying warrior as he asked the spirits to prepare his way for the spirit journey. Quahip's arms and legs began to tremble, as Chama held him to his chest. The words of the song became garbled, until Quahip's last breath whispered from his mouth.

Chama held the body a few moments longer, then he gave the sign of a brave heart in battle and gently put Quahip's head on the grass.

"They will be coming after us," Poke warned, glancing in the direction of the cotton field. "We must hurry."

His face drawn, Conas stood over Quahip.

"We must bury him in the old way. But there is no time. We must leave him here."

Chama walked to one of the ponies and led it over

121

to the body.

"We will take Quahip with us to Palo Duro. Only two more suns. I will not leave him here for the soldiers to find. We will carry him home to the canyon, and bury him in the old way."

Chama took the old Navy Colt from Quahip's belt and held it in front of Taoyo.

"Use this to fight the *Tosi Tivo* if they come again. The spirit of Quahip will be watching. Use it well."

Taoyo took the weapon silently.

"We have only a few bullets," he whispered. "I will be sure of my target before I use the gun."

Chama and Poke lifted Quahip's body to the back of the pony. They tied his hands and feet together under the pony's stomach, as the pony shied nervously at the smell of fresh blood.

With only one spare pony, Chama led the way out of the ravine to a place along the fence. Quickly he jumped down and cut the wires, then he led them through to the west, his heart heavy with sorrow over the death of his friend. One of the last brave Sata Exiponi, who fought the blue coats at Palo Duro, was no longer among them. Quahip's dream of death among the Sata Exiponi had come to pass. He had foreseen his own death in his dream. Chama carried the blame on his shoulders, for it was he who rode out in front to give a warning of danger to the others. He had failed his warriors, and carried the shame of his failure into the night, as he led the way along the twisting course of *Pahehona*. Perhaps, he thought, he had been too certain of Quinne's power and grown careless. As he picked his way through the darkest shadows beneath the trees, he made a promise not to allow himself to grow so careless again.

They hurried the five ponies, worrying about the *Tosi Tivo* from the ambush, stopping often to listen for the sounds of pursuit. Later it became clear no one followed, but with the death of Quahip as a grim reminder of his carelessness, Chama kept a sharp eye on his surroundings until dawn.

They rode to the banks of *Pahehona* at first light. Chama knew the others were tired, and frightened by the encounter with the *Tosi Tivo*. He knew they had to cross the river soon, in order to catch a few hours of rest with the water between them and the soldiers. No matter where they looked, they could find no crossing shallow enough for the ponies. There were no wagon roads, no places where the white men drove their teams across to miss the dangerous sucking sand and deep water. Conas rode up beside Chama, leading the pony bearing Quahip.

"We must cross, Chama. The soldiers will be close. I need a short rest, for the pain grows worse in my bones."

More than any other danger, Chama feared a battle with the soldiers. Four warriors, and only three guns, would do little to stop the charge of the blue-coat cavalry. They must, at all costs, avoid a fight. The death of Quahip only made things worse, with the body tied on the last spare pony. If the soldiers came now with many horses, it would be a short chase before their tired ponies dropped to the ground. Chama knew they must cross the wide river in daylight, to hide their tracks and put the safety of the water between them. But he could find no shallow crossing, and the sucking sands would quickly kill his men and their ponies if

123

they tried to cross without the telltale tracks of the *Tosi Tivo* wagons on the bank.

Chama started along the riverbank, hoping for a crossing to the west, as they rode through the early dawn shadows. Poke's pony had begun to stumble often, worn down from the long ride and weak from hunger. Chama felt the growing danger as he led his warriors beside the river. All the spare ponies were gone, and what was left of them were sore-footed and tired. The most dangerous river of all remained to be crossed, a half-mile of treacherous water and quicksand. He knew the days of freedom could be coming to an end, unless he could find a way to cross the *Pahehona* ahead of the *Tosi Tivo* and the soldiers.

7

Captain Braverman shook his head in disgust, while he listened to Sergeant Hutto's report.

"Nine men are afoot, Cap'n. Three more are leadin' their horses, because they're too lame to carry a rider. Two men passed out in the heat. These boys ain't nothin' but a pack of sissies, if you ask my opinion. We'll never catch up at this rate, sir."

Braverman looked down the column. Some of his men were lying on their backs, complaining of scalded thighs and saddle sores during the rest stop. Grudgingly he was forced to admit that Hutto was right. With more frequent rests demanded by his ailing troopers, they would never catch up with the Indians at all. In this terrible heat, some of the troopers had fallen out of the saddle unconscious. Each mile was leaving a telling effect on the men and horses. Instead of writing a glowing report about his capture of the runaway Comanches, he was faced with the gloomy prospects of a report to his superiors in which Capt. Lloyd Braverman's detail collapsed of heat rash and dizziness, only four days' ride from the fort.

"How far is it to the north fork of the Red River?" he asked, as he wiped his face with a handkerchief.

Hutto unfolded a map and frowned at the paper.

"We should'a been there by now, Cap'n. Maybe just a little farther west."

Braverman gave the order to ride, leading his column across the undulating prairie in the afternoon heat, amid the grumbling complaints of eighty exhausted men, some leading sore-footed horses, while some walked to relieve the searing pain on the insides of their thighs.

An hour later they topped a rise and saw the river. For a moment Lloyd Braverman could not figure out why some of the men behind him were chuckling, until he looked up the river at a group of men and automobiles stranded halfway across the muddy current.

With a sinking feeling in his stomach, Braverman recognized the posse from Mangum, about two dozen men clustered around the half-submerged bodies of their cars. Sheriff Nelson Dobbs stood on the rear seat of one car, barking orders to cursing men as they tried to push the silent machines through the mud. Dobbs waved his arms frantically, pointing this way and that, as he yelled instructions to his men. Profane opinions about Dobbs's advice floated along on a slow summer breeze, while the men grunted and pushed against the hopelessly stuck wheels.

"It seems Mr. Dobbs has a problem," Braverman said, nudging his horse toward the river. Some of the troopers joked and laughed at the posse's plight until their horses entered the shallows.

Braverman rode up beside the first car where Sheriff Dobbs stood, sleeves rolled up and perspiring in the miserable heat. The men from Mangum stopped their futile efforts at moving the buried wheels, staring at the horseback troopers, their faces red from exertion and fatigue.

"By God, I'm glad you fellers came along," Dobbs sighed, wiping his forehead with an arm. "We could use a hand here. I found the tracks of them Apaches where they crossed the river. We came west a ways, to cross in shallow water, but this goddamn mud is deeper than I thought. If you'll hitch a couple of them horses to a rope, we can drag these cars to the other side and be on our way."

Braverman found himself enjoying the moment. He sat his horse without comment for a minute, eyeing the stranded automobiles and the exhausted members of the posse.

"Like I said the other day, Mr. Dobbs, this is army business. We can't stop long enough to give you any assistance. My orders are to stay after the Indians as hard as we can. Best of luck to you, Mr. Dobbs. Hope you get these things out of the river."

Dobbs's chin dropped.

"You mean you ain't gonna help us unstick these cars?"

"Don't have the time," Braverman replied, signaling for his troops to move on.

"Hey!" Dobbs yelled at Braverman's back, as he rode past the cars toward the far bank. "This is an official request from a lawful peace officer to give assistance. By God, sonny, I'll report this to your commanding officer. You can't just ride off and leave us stranded like this! You have to honor an official request, which is what I'm makin' right now. Come back here and toss us a rope."

Braverman did not slow his horse or look back, until his horse trotted out on the riverbank. Only then did he turn to watch as Nelson Dobbs shook his fist in the air at the last of Braverman's column, but the words Dobbs flung at his men were lost in the breeze.

Sergeant Hutto rode past Braverman, wearing a big grin.

"Serves 'em right, Cap'n," Hutto said evenly. "Any man who figures to chase Injuns in one of them contraptions has got rocks in his head."

Braverman pushed his men through the heat of the morning. At noon he called a halt, and allowed the men an hour's rest to eat a cold lunch of crackers and tinned tomatoes. Men sprawled in the shade, leaving their horses to wander and graze, too tired and sore to give proper care to their mounts.

"Assemble the men after their meal," Braverman said crisply, as Hutto chewed his tasteless lunch. "I'm not going to have my men embarrass me to Major Townsend. I plan to set them straight on a few things."

Hutto shook his head.

"They're just green kids, Cap'n. A few drills don't get a man ready to ride this long and sleep on the ground. These men ain't in shape to chase Injuns, sir. We'll be down to a crawl by tomorrow, with half our horses gone lame."

Braverman clamped his jaw, angry at the turn of events that was about to rob him of a transfer from

128

Fort Sill.

"Assemble the men, Sergeant."

Hutto brought the sunburnt troops to attention in a ragged line in front of Captain Braverman. A few looked too weak to stand in the oppressive heat, leaning against each other like men who were near complete collapse.

"Men," Braverman began sternly, "I want you to listen closely. This duty is perhaps the most important you've had in your military careers. We must find these Indians. It is very important that each one of you gives me one hundred percent of your efforts. We are on the trail of fifty murderers. If we handle this assignment well, it could mean a commendation for each one of you. I want all this grumbling to stop at once. We are soldiers, performing our duty. Are there any questions?"

Braverman glared up and down the line, daring anyone to ask a question.

"Then let's get mounted. There will be no more rest stops until we've sighted those Indians."

Chama waited in a grove of trees as the wagon rolled out on the riverbank. A whip cracked above the squeak of wheels as the freight wagon rolled away from the river. At last they had found a crossing, a white man's wagon road. Blowflies buzzed noisily over Quahip's body as the sounds of the wagon faded in the distance, feeding on the dried blood as Chama urged his pony toward the river crossing.

He guided his pony into the shallows. Mud sucked at

129

the ponies' hooves, making a struggle out of each step as they walked the tired ponies over the half-mile of slow current to the far side.

Chama turned and watched the north bank for a moment. The crossing went without trouble. They were alone on the banks of *Pahehona*. Their back trail was clear.

He led at a walk to the south, leaving sight of the river before he selected a grove of trees. They dropped off the ponies and hobbled them, then stretched out under the shading limbs for a few hours of badly needed sleep. Chama knew they should keep a guard, to watch for the soldiers, but all his warriors were too exhausted to stay awake. They lay on the cool grass after four days and nights without sleep, and were soon deep in dreamless slumber, while the ponies grazed not far away. A swarm of blowflies came to feed on the stiffening corpse, buzzing angrily over the dried blood and putrid flesh slung over the back of one pony. But like the other animals, the pony was too hungry to notice as it moved from one bunch of grass to the next, hobbling on sore hooves with a single purpose . . . finding enough food to stay alive.

The soft snorting of a pony awakened Chama suddenly. He reached for the rifle beside him, and found it missing from the spot where he left it. He sat up and looked around the camp, worried by the sound from the pony, until he saw Taoyo at the edge of the trees with Chama's rifle in the crook of one arm.

Chama got up and walked through the trees toward the boy. Taoyo was awake, standing watch over their back trail beside the thick trunk of a gnarled oak.

130

"No one comes," the boy whispered. "There is no dust sign on the horizon."

Chama sat beside Taoyo, scanning the skyline carefully before he spoke.

"You have done well, Taoyo. For a boy of so few taums, you have the courage of a warrior."

The boy did not look at Chama when he replied.

"I was frightened when the *Tosi Tivo* shot at us in the dark. I have tried to drive the fear from my heart, but it will not leave. A warrior is not afraid, Toyah Chama. I am still only a boy in my heart. I have thought of Quahip all day, and when I think about the *Tosi Tivo* bullets killing Quahip, I am afraid. There is nothing I can do to make the fear leave me."

Chama squinted at the horizon, remembering a time long past when he was a boy, longing for the day when he might become a warrior like his father.

"When I was young, I was afraid of many things. Each taum, Powva sent many tests of my courage. As I grew older, I began to understand why I was afraid. My fear gave me strength to fight harder, to become stronger than my fear. To be afraid is a good thing when the enemy is near. You will have the strength of two warriors in battle."

Taoyo kept his eyes on the ground.

"My grandfather told me only women are afraid of death."

Chama turned to the boy and poked a finger in the dirt.

"When you are older, you will understand what it means to die and walk to the spirit world. There are places on mother earth much worse than the land of departed spirits. One place is the white man's reservation. Life as a prisoner of the white men is worth nothing to a Comanche. For only a few days, Quahip knew the old freedom of his people. His walk toward the spirit world will be a happy journey, remembering his last days on mother earth riding his pony across the great prairies. It is much better to die a free man, than to walk in chains as a prisoner of the white man's law. If we die fighting for our freedom, it is a better way than death at Fort Sill."

For some time Taoyo gazed silently at the gentle swells of the prairie, remembering the stories told by Buffalo Hump and Pohawcut about the Kwahadies and the other Comanche tribes, from the days before they came to Fort Sill.

"When I was small," Taoyo began, "my grandfather would hold me on his knee and tell me stories, about the canyons . . . the Palo Duro, and Pena Pah. In the beginning, I did not understand the sadness in his voice. I wondered why the water came to his eyes when he told me the stories. Pohawcut cried when she heard him tell me about wild ponies and the buffalo. One night, I heard my grandfather chant the prayers to Powva, then he stopped and began to cry. He asked Powva to forgive him for laying down his rifle at Palo Duro, in the battle with the soldiers. His voice was shaking. He begged the great spirit for the strength to rise from his blankets, to fight the soldiers again. I could not understand why the freedom he talked about was so important, for I was born on the reservation. I did not know what this word 'freedom' meant, because the teachers at the school taught us that we were a free people in America. But now, riding with you, Toyah Chama, I understand why my grandfather cried. Out here, riding the ponies wherever we wish to go, without the boundaries of the fort, I think I understand the word 'freedom.' We can go any place we choose, without the permission of Tatum or the blue coats."

Chama watched the boy's face, feeling a trace of water come to his eyes. He stood up and walked to the edge of the grove, feeling the heat as he left the shaded ground beneath the limbs. He stood, gazing at the empty horizon, watching the wind blow wavy patterns through the dry grass.

Taoyo came to stand beside him. Chama pointed to the prairie and the distant outlines of bigger hills and buttes to the west.

"Once there were so many buffalo and deer, our people knew no hunger. In your grandfather's time, we followed the buffalo and built our lodges near the streams and rivers. The People were happy. They knew of no other life than the open plains. When the *Tosi Tivo* came, we fought them, defending our land. For many taums the white men left us alone, knowing we could defeat them in battle. Then so many came we could not win battles, but we did not stop fighting. We struck their farms at night and drove their cattle away, to show the *Tosi Tivo* we would defend our homes with our lives. Then the soldiers came, and we left the plains to hide in Palo Duro and Pena Pah. Still, the blue-coat soldiers came, hunting us in the canyons, attacking our villages, killing the women and children. Then they sent Mackenzie and all his soldiers to find us in Pena Pah. War Chief Quannah and your grandfather fought

133

with every warrior, until our bullets and arrows were gone. Buffalo Hump and Quannah stopped fighting, to save the women and children. It was the only thing left. Our chiefs could not watch the children die any longer."

Chama knelt in the dry grass and held it in his fingers.

"I tried to keep the word of The People given in the treaty. For eighteen taums I sat at the soldier fort with my weapons in the ground, watching the white men starve my people and give them the crazy water to sicken their spirits. At night I said the prayers to Powva, asking Him to let my people go free. But with every taum, more of The People died, of the white man's sickness and from hunger. I waited, saying the old prayers, begging Powva for a sign that would show me a way to save my people, but there was no sign."

Chama turned to the boy and placed a hand on his shoulder.

"A day came when I lost all hope. I believed Powva had turned His back on His people, because they chose the white man's road. I made ready to leave the fort alone. I chose death over the way the *Tosi Tivo* kept us on the reservation. I came to the bluff west of the fort one last time to seek a spirit sign, and Quinne came to the skies above my head. You know the power of the eagle sign. In my spirit I knew the soldiers could not stop me with the power of Quinne to protect me. Your grandfather understood. He knew Quinne would lead us safely from the fort. In two more suns, we will be in Palo Duro. The soldiers may come, but they will not stop us, if we fight with all our courage. You are a warrior now, Taoyo. You must fight with all your strength if the blue coats come close. But it will be worth any price to live as free Comanches. When you see the Pena Pah, it will help you understand why your grandfather wanted you to come with me."

Taoyo met Chama's eyes with a silent look, his face filled with determination. He pulled Quahip's pistol from his belt and held it at his side.

"I will fight," he whispered, "even as I fear the *Tosi Tivo* bullets. I will do nothing to take honor from the name of my grandfather."

Chama walked among the sleeping warriors, awakening them with a gentle nudge. They caught the ponies and rode away from their camp feeling better, still turning often to watch the skyline for sign of the soldiers, as they pushed westward through the heat of the day.

Taoyo's pony was suddenly lame, lifting a foreleg to hop painfully over the ground. The boy dropped off quickly and picked up the hoof, examining it for a sharp stone or a cut. As Chama joined him to look at the hoof, Taoyo found a jagged cut along the tender frog at the back of the foot, seeping blood onto Taoyo's palm.

"The pony is finished," Chama said, as he pulled the rawhide loop from the pony's mouth. The little brown mare hobbled to a patch of grass and began grazing.

"I will walk," Taoyo said, shouldering his waterskin. "I can keep up. I will lead Quahip's pony."

Taoyo took the rein and pulled the pony to a place in

line behind Conas, as Chama started toward a lowering sun in the distance. The body had begun to stink, swarming with blowflies as the pony walked.

Chama knew the ponies were too weak for another run. If the soldiers came, they would have no choice but to pick a spot where they could fight. In only one more sun, they would be in sight of Palo Duro, but the shuffling gait of his pony warned that the distance might be too great for their worn mounts.

The summer sun baked their skin, adding to the difficulty for the laboring ponies. Poke could not force his pony into a slow trot, even when he slapped his rifle barrel on the pony's rump. Chama held a straight course over the empty prairie, no longer hiding their passage in scattered trees, saving the ponies as many steps as he could be traveling in a straight line.

At sunset they rode down a slope to a shallow stream. Conas slid from his pony's back and cupped water in his hands, while the ponies drank their fill.

"We are near," Conas said, his face drawn tight with the pain filling his body. "One more sun, Chama. I can see the rise of the hills in the distance."

Chama was looking at the dim outlines of several flat buttes below the setting sun.

"We will see Palo Duro with tomorrow's sun," he sighed.

Poke gathered the rein on his pony and shook his head.

"This pony will not last another day, Chama. We should leave Quahip here and ride the best ponies. It will only take a short time to dig his grave."

Chama turned suddenly, eyes fixed on Poke.

136

"I will not leave our Kwahadie brother for the soldiers. Tie Quahip on the back of the weak pony. Quahip will sleep in the ground of our fathers."

It was a grisly task, untying the stiff corpse to move it to another pony. Conas could not help them, too weak from the pain in his joints to do anything but sit beside the stream. Taoyo helped until the smell filled his nose, then he turned away, choking up a bellyful of water, unable to stop the gagging reflex brought on by the putrid flesh.

When they finished, they mounted again, Taoyo trotting with the rein over his shoulder, pulling the weakest pony along to keep up with the rest. At a steady walk they rode through the first shadows of night, pushing men and ponies beyond their limits over the rolling grassland.

They were forced to rest often during the night, allowing the ponies more time to graze and regain their strength. Chama could see the trembling weakness beginning in the legs of two ponies, a warning that the little horses were at the end of their endurance. In a few hours, the ponies could go no further.

At dawn Chama led them to the bank of the river. All night his warriors held a grim silence, for each knew how close they were to the last faltering steps of the ponies.

Conas rode his pony into the shallows and tumbled from its back, splashing as he fell on the glassy surface. He came up on his knees in the muddy water, eyes closed with pain, his bronze cheeks a chalky white.

"I can ride no more, Chama," he groaned, gritting his teeth while his limbs shook with fatigue. "You must

137

take the others and go on. I will lie here in this cool water until the soldiers come. Leave me the old pistol. I will fight, and make the blue coats wait to find me. Leave me here, and hurry to the canyon."

Chama dropped off his pony and waded through the water to Conas.

"You are a Sata Exiponi. We are the strong among our people. We must show the others at Fort Sill that the soldiers could not stop us. Only this last day, and we will be home."

Conas shook his head and sat down in the mud.

"I am too weak, Chama. I will die bravely here, fighting the blue coats. Go on without me."

Chama bent down to lift Conas by the arms. Taoyo ran into the water and helped Chama pull Conas to his feet.

"I will not leave you," Taoyo said, a plea in his thin voice. "You saved my life in the river. If you stay, I will stay with you to fight the soldiers."

Chama swept them with a fiery look.

"No one stays! We are very close!"

Conas fell heavily against Chama and slipped back down on his knees.

"I cannot ride, Chama. The pain is too great in my bones."

Chama looked down on the pleading eyes of his old friend, and felt the strength returning in his limbs.

"Do you remember the drinking place among the rocks in Pena Pah? Do you remember how sweet the water tastes in the pool? It is cool, and as sweet as the honey of the bees. Remember, Conas, and hold the memory in your heart as you sit on the pony. At the end

138

of one more day, you will be in Palo Duro."

Conas turned and gazed to the west, as sunlight bathed the landscape with early yellow glow. He squinted at the distant buttes and began a soft chant to the four spirits, asking for strength in his limbs.

Conas finished his prayer and started to rise, his mouth set in a hard line.

"Help me to my pony," he groaned as he came to his feet, swaying, unable to stand without assistance from the boy. "I will ride until I fall, or until the pony falls under me."

Chama and Taoyo lifted Conas to his pony's back. Conas wrapped a gnarled hand in the pony's mane and took the rein.

"Hurry, Chama, before my hand grows too weak to keep me on the pony's back. I can feel the soldier horses coming, so many they shake the ground."

Chama led away from the river at a walk, keeping to the trees wherever he could, saving the ponies' strength by avoiding the burning rays of the sun. He stopped often to let the ponies rest and nibble grass. Chama's pony had begun to limp, its little hooves worn down to the quick, broken and splitting at the heels.

More often than ever, Chama turned back to watch for the soldiers, for like Conas, he could feel the soldier horses drawing nearer as their own progress slowed.

By mid-afternoon Chama's pony was too sore to carry a rider. He dropped to the ground and led the animal behind him, searching the distance for a sign of the high walls of the mouth of Palo Duro canyon. But in the haze above the horizon, he saw only the flat buttes and hills of the day before.

Suddenly, Poke's pony began to cough. Poke jumped off and stood beside the pony, untying his waterskin and the last of their deer meat. The bay gelding lowered its head and coughed foamy blood from its nose, with its legs spread wide to remain standing.

"Another pony is finished, Chama," Poke said softly. "I will walk beside Taoyo."

Chama glanced worriedly to the east. Only one pony remained that was strong enough to carry a rider. Conas clung to his pony's back, his face twisted in pain. The pony bearing Quahip's body was trembling from weakness. Chama's pony was too lame to carry any weight. If the soldiers came now, there was no chance to escape them, or reach the safety of the canyon hiding places.

Chama looked west. He blinked, and tried to focus on a faint shape in the haze above the horizon. The longer he looked at the shape, the more certain he became. It was the mouth of Palo Duro canyon, the towering rock cliffs marking the entrance to the winding canyons that followed the course of *Pahehona*.

"Look!" he cried, pointing with a trembling finger. "I can see the great canyon."

For a silent moment the others followed Chama's finger to the purple outline of the canyon mouth.

Taoyo jumped with excitement.

"I can see it, too! It is very close!"

Conas tried to find the spot, his eyes filling with watery tears.

"My eyes are too old. Hurry, Chama. Lead the way

140

closer, so my old eyes can look on our homeland once again."

Poke shaded his eyes from the sun, then he turned to watch the horizon behind them.

"I will walk beside Conas and hold him on his pony. Go quickly, Chama. We must reach the canyon before dark."

They left the dying pony as it coughed more blood and went to its knees. Poke thought of the trail of dead or crippled ponies they were leaving behind, marking their trail as plainly as any hoofprint for the soldiers to follow, as he walked beside Conas through the dried grass. Then he fixed his eyes on the hazy canyon walls in front of them, and walked silently behind Chama to the west.

8

Sam stood in the stirrups as the buckskin trotted through a dry wash and out to the other side before it slowed to a walk. Sam mumbled another string of cuss-words, directed toward his throbbing knees, as he settled back in the saddle. All night long he had cussed his joints, unable to find a comfortable place on his bedroll where the pain did not keep him awake. In the soft light of morning, there was a beauty to this part of Texas, something he might have enjoyed were it not for the pain. It had been a long hot ride from Childress, yet at the same time, the ride filled him with an inner peace, a soothing reminder of days gone by, when he rode the open ranges as a marshal, without the damnable ache in his joints.

This morning, quite by accident, he found the tracks of the Comanches. Walking through a grove of live oak to relieve himself at dawn, he found unshod hoofprints and the remains of a burned-out campfire. Since first light, he and Tom had followed the tracks, moving unerringly west, south of the river. It was a fancy piece of luck, and an unbelievable find. Chama and his men had miraculously come better than three hundred miles. There were now fewer tracks to follow, only five barefooted ponies leaving prints in the red clay near the river.

Something, or someone, had thinned the ranks of Chama's horses. It could be simple wear and tear, as the thin ponies played out after so much distance. Or, it could mean a fight had been lost, somewhere north of the river in Oklahoma. Fewer tracks could mean fewer surviving Indians. But at the dead campfire, Sam was sure he found four sets of moccasin tracks in the dry ground. From the looks of things, all five could have survived the three hundred miles of fences and farms into Texas. It was hard to tell on sun-baked ground, but he thought he could make out five sets of prints around the campfire. If nothing else, it was a tribute to the toughness of the five men and their scrawny horses, coming so far through armed posses and settled country. It was nothing short of amazing, how Chama could find his way back after almost twenty years.

Sam reined the buckskin to the top of a grassy knoll and pulled his field glasses from his saddlebags. For some time he scanned the horizon carefully, moving the glasses slowly until he found what he was looking for. In the soft haze along the skyline he focused on a towering wall of limestone, so faint in the distance that it bore no detail, but Sam was certain it was the opening that marked the beginnings of the Palo Duro canyon. The top of the limestone cliff stretched beyond the range of his glasses, but if he remembered correctly, the butte was the entrance to a maze of offshoot canyons leading away from the Red River. For better

144

than fifty rugged miles, the Red ran a crooked course through the limestone to the headwaters where the river began. It was some of the roughest country in the southwest, deep chasms with straight walls running down to the river, some over five hundred feet high, with a sheer drop of craggy limestone.

While Sam put away the glasses, he wondered how far in front of them the Comanches might be. Judging by the tracks, and the feel of the dead campfire, Chama was half a day or more ahead. One of the ponies was lame in a foreleg, making a distinctly different print as it tried to keep weight from a sore hoof. A lame pony would slow them down considerably, enough so that he and Tom might close the gap to a few hours, if they rode hard.

"Can you see anything?" Tom asked, standing in his stirrups.

"Wasn't expectin' to," Sam replied. "If a man sees Comanches, it's only because they want him to. I doubt we'll see anything until their horses play out, if we find 'em at all."

They rode off the knoll, following the faint tracks on a course almost due west. Chama was making no effort to hide his tracks, with a lame pony and no spare horses. He was headed straight as an arrow for the canyon, no longer worrying about the signs of his passing.

As they crossed a ridge, Sam noticed buzzards floating in the breeze a few miles away. He touched his horse with a spur, wondering if the birds were circling the handful of Indians, certain that the few men and crippled ponies could not last long in the oppressive heat.

145

When they found the pony, it was still alive, lying on its side, too weak to rise as the ugly black buzzards perched on its ribs, waiting for the struggle to end. The buzzards had already pecked out the pony's eyes, choice morsels for the carrion, as the pony gasped for breath around the bloody foam in its throat, too feeble to fight off the swarming vultures.

Sam rode up and scattered the birds, borrowing Tom's pistol to put the pony out of its misery with a bullet. As a man who loved horses, he could not leave the little horse to die slowly, even though the echo of the gunshot might warn the Comanches that someone was close behind.

"Pitiful sight, ain't it?" Sam sighed, as he handed Tom his pistol. "A horse that thin ain't supposed to be carryin' a rider, even a skinny Indian. Damn shame, how the army starved their horses. Ought to be a law against it. Times, I think ol' Tatum does all his thinkin' with his ass. How could anybody starve a horse like this?"

Tom turned away and holstered his gun.

"Most of the Indians at Fort Sill aren't in much better shape. I've been out there a time or two when Tatum gives them their rations. A hungry coyote wouldn't touch that flour, crawlin' with weevils and worms."

"The beef ain't any better," Sam said, climbing back in his saddle. "I can smell it when they open the locker. Probably as old as I am."

Sam studied the tracks around the dead pony, reading the sign in the dirt. The lame pony was still in the bunch. Chama was exhausting his supply of horses. The chase was nearing an end.

146

"Let's keep after them tonight," Sam sighed, thinking of his aching bones. "I can't find a way to sleep on this hard ground anyways. Might as well spend the night in a saddle. I can't sleep either way."

They rode off toward a lowering sun, feeling the heat soak their shirts to sweating skin. It was no surprise that Chama's ponies were falling apart. Even the grain-fed horses from Childress were beginning to suffer in the summer heat.

Tom rode alongside Sam, pulling off his hat to wipe sweat from his eyes as the horses trotted up a gradual incline. In the distance they could see a change in the land, an end to the soft grasses where slabs of rock jutted out of the ground. The iron horseshoes began to click over the uneven surface, as piles of loose stones littered their path. They noticed the lighter green color of thorny mesquite trees in the distance. A hot wind had begun from the west, gusting as it blew in their faces. Tom's black gelding began to puff through its nose with the effort of their climb toward the buttes. As the heat of the day began to build, Sam felt a swelling in his right boot, as his ankle filled with fluid.

Sam found a shady grove and rode toward it, stopping beneath the sheltering trees to ease down from the saddle. When his right foot touched the ground, a sharp stab of pain went up his leg.

"Damn that hurts," he mumbled, loosening the girth on his buckskin before he sat down under an elm tree. "Let's eat one of Clara's biscuits and rest a spell. My right foot is killin' me."

Tom hobbled the horses and unpacked Sam's bedroll. He gave Sam a biscuit and brought a canteen, then he sat beside Sam in the shade while they ate, glancing now and then at the mouth of Palo Duro in the distance.

"I've been thinkin'," Tom said around a mouthful of bread, "that this whole business is a big waste of the taxpayer's money. There's the two of us, and God knows how many soldiers, spending all this time just to track down four men who really didn't commit a crime. They just wandered off peacefully, as far as we know. I can't figure out why our Fort Smith office wanted us to get involved in the first place. Seems like we've got better things to do back in Cache. I can think of two murder warrants we've got on the desk, and there's the investigation of the bank robbery in Leedy we haven't finished yet."

Sam tried to pull off his boot, but the swelling had tightened it around his ankle, and he was forced to give up.

"Charlie just read the newspapers," Sam sighed heavily. "I should have wired him a true account of things much sooner, but I never dreamed the papers would make such a big fuss. Ike Tatum wanted big headlines, and he damn sure got 'em. I read the story in the Childress paper, while you were gone to rent the horses."

"I sent Fort Smith a telegram, like you said, telling them it was only four old men and a boy. Maybe they'll contact the Bureau of Indian Affairs in Washington and set things straight on the Indian uprising. This thing could backfire in Ike Tatum's face, if the Bureau investigates the matter."

Sam shook his head sadly.

"You don't understand the way a bureaucracy works, Tom. It could take months, maybe even years,

148

for all the reports to get to the right places. It would serve Tatum right if the Bureau started an investigation as to why every damn soldier at Fort Sill was sent out to look for five runaway Indians. But my experience with Washington makes me believe the whole thing will just blow over after a spell. Tatum will get what he wants, the big headlines and plenty of attention. I doubt if anybody at the Bureau of Indian Affairs gives a damn anyway."

Tom gazed thoughtfully at the horizon a moment.

"We could send them a wire, telling the whole story. It might make a difference. Maybe Tatum would have to explain his actions to his superiors."

Sam nodded, a grin creasing his face.

"Good idea, Tom. It'll be too late to make things any easier for Chama, but it might make Tatum think twice before he pulled this stunt again."

Tom sipped from his canteen, then he came to his feet.

"Once Chama gets inside that big canyon, he's gonna be pretty hard to find. It could take weeks to track him down."

Sam frowned as he remembered the rocky passages twisting the length of Palo Duro.

"A man might not ever find them, Tom. On rocky ground, a little pony, maybe eight or nine hundred pounds, don't leave much for a man to follow when it comes to tracks. If you put a Comanche on his back—an old warrior who knows how to hide his trail—it could be damn near impossible to follow him."

Tom looked down on Sam's sun-browned face, for he had heard the indecision again in Sam's voice.

"Would it make any difference to you if we couldn't

149

find them?" Tom asked.

Sam looked up quickly, wondering about Tom's motives for asking the question.

"Why do you ask, Tom?"

Tom flashed a wide grin as he walked away to his horse.

"It's my guess you really hope we don't find Chama at all. I ain't sayin' you won't look mighty hard, but I don't think you'll be disappointed if we can't locate them in that canyon."

Sam started to protest, but Tom was not listening any longer, as he walked out in the sunlit grass to catch Sam's hobbled horse.

There was a terrible truth in Tom's observations about the search for Chama. For the first time in over forty years, Sam found himself moving closer to a moment of decision he dreaded. If they found Chama, Sam could not be sure he had the stomach for arresting him and the others to haul them back to Fort Sill. The farther they rode west, the more his resolve softened, until he now doubted his commitment to upholding the law which required Chama's return. For two days he had wrestled with himself on the silent prairie, thinking how wrong it would seem to take the old men back to the stench and flies of Fort Sill in manacles. Again and again he found himself wondering what he would do, if the moment arrived when Chama must be taken prisoner. The more he thought about it, the less certain he became that he could honor the oath taken when he first pinned on a marshal's badge, to uphold the laws of the United States and do his duty. This was one duty he had come to dread, for in his heart he felt sympathy for the old Comanches, no matter what the law said.

Also, it was not likely that Chama would give up without a fight. When they had talked, back on the bluff overlooking the fort, Chama's voice betrayed him. He would rather die than face another year at Fort Sill. And Sam knew he would not be the one who fired a bullet into Chama for his attempt to remain free in Texas. No matter how often Sam thought about it—his duty and the responsibilities that came with his badge—he knew he could not kill Chama, or any of the rest of them.

Sam tried to stand up, but the pain in his right foot almost drove him to the ground. By hanging on to a tree trunk, he pulled himself upright, letting loose a string of angry cusswords as he tried to balance on his good ankle.

Tom went to his saddlebags and removed a pint of whiskey.

"I brought this along. It'll probably do more for your disposition than your arthritis, but I'd give it a try if I was you."

Sam took the bottle, grinning in spite of his pain.

"Damned if I know what to do about you, Deputy Ford. One part of me says it's time to give you a raise, for bringing along this whiskey. But the other half of me says you ought to be fired right away, for waiting two whole days before you told me about it."

He took a big swallow, feeling the fiery burn down his throat as the whiskey went to his belly.

"I feel better already," Sam hissed, tucking the bottle inside his shirt. "I guess I'll keep you on for a while. You ain't been fired just yet, but you're on dangerous ground if you're hidin' another bottle in those saddlebags."

They mounted and rode off into the heat, holding a jogging trot over the rocks and bunchgrass, as the land rose gently toward the buttes.

Tom turned back in the saddle to speak, shouting above the hot wind building on the prairie.

"If it puts your mind to rest, I kind'a hope we don't find Chama myself. A man tough enough to ride this far, just so he can breathe a little fresh air, he deserves to get where he's going, even if it's only for a little while."

9

He walked between the sheer cliffs of the canyon leading his limping pony. He did not feel the pain in his feet, even though the rough climb to the entrance over sharp stones had torn one of his moccasins and left one foot bleeding. The ache in his tired muscles was gone, replaced by a wonderful feeling, as if his heart had the wings of an eagle, as he walked through the mouth of Palo Duro canyon, returning home after eighteen of the longest years of his life. Behind him the others began to chant, praising Powva for bringing them safely home. He heard Conas above the rest, his quivering voice a mournful cry of happiness, echoing off the rock cliffs, bouncing back from every corner of the canyon, a sound so plaintive it sent a chill down Chama's spine.

He stopped and turned to his warriors.

"Quinne's medicine was strong. We are home at last, my brothers. We are the last free warriors on the face of mother earth. Say the prayers of thanks. We will die here as free men. The soldiers will not find us now."

153

Conas slid from his pony and fell on the limestone, singing his prayers in a choking voice, while tears streamed down his face.

"Our long journey is over," Poke cried, raising his arms to the rocky cliffs, beginning another chant of thanksgiving.

Taoyo turned his head from one sheer rock cliff to the next, for even the stories of his grandfather did not prepare him for the size of the canyon. Canyon walls towered above them on both sides of the river, stretching into the distance following the westward course of *Pahehona*.

Chama looked up the canyon, remembering the trails he would follow. To the north, several miles up the river, was the hidden entrance to the *Habbe Taniharro*, only a narrow slice in the rock wide enough for a pony to squeeze through, named for the beautiful wildflowers which grew along the path. It was near the top of *Habbe Taniharro*, in a sheltered pocket overlooking the river far below, that Chama would bury Quahip. For the rest of time, Quahip would see the canyon with his earth-body, while his spirit walked the windswept canyon trails.

Then Chama would lead his warriors to *Habbe Pia*, a secret warrior's path twisting through the limestone cliffs for a great distance, finally leading to the hidden canyon called Pena Pah.

Chama examined the river, low in the dry summer and easy to cross. Along the banks, thick stands of grass grew, and spiked cholla plants among the rocks fallen from the high cliffs. It was a beauty he had dreamed about for eighteen taums, an empty place

154

filled with the bounty of mother earth. Chama felt water in his eyes as he looked up the winding canyon. His spirit would find peace at last. There would be no more tortured dreams to haunt him, dim memories of what it was like to ride his pony along the Comanche trails in Palo Duro. He would ride the trails again. It would no longer be only a dream.

Suddenly, he was aware of the danger for himself and his warriors, standing in plain sight in the mouth of the canyon. He turned quickly to the east, studying the hroizon carefully for a sign of the soldiers.

He moved his eyes slowly, until they stopped on a distant speck, a dark spot against a chalky rise in the bald prairie.

"Someone comes," Chama said hoarsely, pointing a finger. "It will be scouts for the soldiers. Come quickly."

Poke shaded his eyes as Taoyo helped Conas on his pony.

"I see them now. They are only a few, but they will show the blue coats our tracks."

Chama picked up the rein and led his pony to the banks of the river. He waded into the shallow current, feeling sharp stones through his worn moccasins, as he walked across the river to a slab of limestone on the north bank. He waited until the others made the crossing safely through the waist-deep water, then Chama turned west and started along the rockiest ground beside the river, careful to hide their tracks as well as he could in their haste.

They walked to the first bend in the canyon walls, where the river swung south, then west again. Chama began searching the cliff for the tiny slice into the rock that became *Habbe Taniharro*. In his heart he knew he could find the spot, but as they walked farther along the river, he began to worry. So many taums had passed since he last walked the Palo Duro. Floods and falling rock seemed to have changed the canyon floor, for he found little he remembered as he led his pony at a fast walk below the cliffs.

He turned often to watch for the scouts, wondering if they would be the Lipan Apaches Mackenzie used to track the Kwahadies before. Without the Lipans, Mackenzie's soldiers would never have found the Comanches in the canyons, for it took another Indian to know the ways of hiding tracks on rocky ground.

The bare hooves of the ponies echoed off the canyon walls as the passage narrowed. Chama's feet were sore and bleeding, leaving a telltale trail of blood on the limestone through his worn moccasins. The pony bearing Quahip began to stumble, its hooves too sore for the sharp stones under its feet. Chama looked carefully for the opening, and still he could not find it as they walked deeper into the Palo Duro.

The sun dropped below the canyon walls, painting the canyon floor with shadows. Birds flew from their path, frightened quail and sparrows. An armadillo scurried away in the grass. Chama tried to hurry his pony, but the animal could not travel faster than a walk on sore hooves.

At a turn in the canyon, Chama saw the crevice, half-hidden by a tangle of mesquites and cholla. He almost ran to the spot, pushing limbs aside to peer up at the sharp climb through a solid wall of limestone toward the rim of the canyon. For almost twenty taums, only deer and wild animals used the slender passage to the top. Dry grass grew thickly in the passage, untouched by the feet of men for so long, a secret known only to the Comanches who had once made the Palo Duro their home.

He and the boy pulled the brush away from the opening, then Chama led his pony into the crevice and began the hard, straight climb away from the canyon floor. He slipped often, losing his footing. Behind him the pony scrambled to keep its feet under it, until Chama reached a level spot where he stopped to wait for the others.

Poke was last into the passage, piling brush in front of the opening, then sweeping their tracks away with a mesquite limb as he backed slowly upward. Then he tossed the limb aside and hurried to catch up, struggling in the steepest places on torn moccasins.

Chama resumed the climb, twisting around sharp turns between rock walls, passing through tight places barely wide enough for a pony. Conas clung to his pony's mane, his face tight with pain, summoning all his strength to stay on the pony's back.

It was a climb filled with memories for Chama. As a boy he had run up and down this trail with a short bow and little dogwood arrows, trying in vain to kill rabbits or a fox, playing games with other Kwahadie children as he dreamed of the day when he would be old enough to become a warrior. These were some of the happiest memories of his life, coming back with each turn in the trail, as he wound his way toward a slice of evening sky at the top of the walls over his head.

At a bend in the trail Chama stopped, waiting for Taoyo to climb up behind him. As worn and tired as they were, the climb was draining the last strength from the men and ponies. Chama's sides heaved from the effort, and his feet ached from the sharp stones littering the bottom of the trail.

When the others were in sight, he continued more slowly as weakness trembled down his legs. He was suddenly dizzy and had to keep one hand against the rock to prevent a fall. He knew the others were in no better shape, but a glance toward the rim made new energy surge through his limbs. The top was just a short distance away.

Rounding a sharp turn, Chama walked into the pocket overlooking the canyon floor. Near the edge was a thin layer of soil where wildflowers grew in the spring, a fitting resting place for Quahip, marked by the beauty of mother earth.

Chama led his pony to level ground and fell on the grass, exhausted and dizzy, unable to walk another step. He heard the others walking toward him, but he was too weak to lift his head from the soft dry grass.

Taoyo helped Conas to lie down beside Chama. Poke began untying the swollen corpse, sending a swarm of flies into the air as he carried Quahip to the edge of the rim.

"I will dig the grave," Taoyo said softly, as Poke staggered over to the others to rest on the grass. While the ponies grazed, Taoyo began scraping away the soil with a sharp stone. Chama could do nothing to help, sucking air into his lungs, waiting for the dizziness to leave him. After a short rest, Poke got up and helped the boy finish a shallow grave, resting on his knees as he

158

scraped away loose soil.

Chama pushed himself up, arms trembling, then he walked unsteadily to the body and helped the others move it into the hole. They covered Quahip gently, unable to look at his swollen face and blackened limbs, until he rested beneath the soil at the edge of the canyon.

For a short time they rested, until Chama began chanting an old prayer for the departed spirit of a brave warrior. The others joined the chant, their voices cracked and thin, carried away by a gentle breeze flowing through the canyon as night fell on Palo Duro.

Chama stared across the canyon at the southern rim in the fading light, allowing a silent moment to pass when the prayer was finished. His thoughts were filled with memories of his friend Quahip, of a lifetime as a companion to the body resting in front of him. It was a sad moment, knowing Quahip had not lived long enough to see the Palo Duro and Pena Pah. A *Tosi Tivo* bullet robbed Quahip of his reward for the dangerous escape from Fort Sill. There was only the knowledge that he found a few days of freedom in their run from the fort before the bullet came.

"We will come back," Chama said softly, "when the soldiers leave. We can sing the songs of happiness above his resting place. But now, there is no time. We must hurry to hide our tracks from the scouts."

They caught their ponies and followed the *Habbe Taniharro* toward the top, the trail darkened with nightfall. From the pocket the trail was easier to climb, turning often before it led to the top of the canyon.

Chama led out on level ground, feeling a sharp wind from the west, a cool movement of air carrying the smell of rain. A bank of clouds covered the stars to the northwest. He heard the distant rumble of thunder.

Chama raised his arms to the sky, for in his heart he knew why the rain was coming. Powva was sending water to strengthen the grasses in Pena Pah, to fatten the ponies and deer for the winter. The Comanches would have food for their winter lodges, and strong ponies to ride as they hid from the soldiers. Powva had declared an end to the long dry season, preparing the hidden canyon for His people, so that they would live as they had long ago, at peace to enjoy the bounty of mother earth. In spite of his aching feet, he walked faster, remembering a sheltering cave in a basin several miles to the west where they could cook the last of their deer meat and wait for the storm to pass.

Sam sat his horse in the last rays of evening light, looking up the mouth of Palo Duro canyon.

"Looks like they made it, Tom. I suppose I'm glad they did. It'd be a damn shame to ride so hard and come so far to come up a few miles short."

"What'll we do now?" Tom asked, feeling a gust of wind tug at his hat.

Sam leaned an elbow on his saddlehorn, as he examined the canyon walls stretching in front of them.

"Ain't much choice. We've got to make a try at finding them. I reckon you know my heart ain't gonna be in it, but we'll have to try. This thing is a lesson for both of us. If a man wants something bad enough, no matter how the odds stack up against him, he can do it if he tries hard enough. It's downright unnatural how ol' Chama could come this far like he did. It defies all

160

the laws of nature. A starved horse and a seventy-year-old man can't cover four hundred miles of barbed wire and gun-totin' posses in six days, but he did it anyway. Most men his age can't get out of a rockin' chair without help, an' he just swings bareback on a half-dead pony and rides four hundred miles. To get this far, they've had to ride day and night, and they've done it on little horses so damn weak they couldn't pull a man's hat off his head in a high wind. Unshod horses to boot. For the life of me, I can't figure out how they made it, but tracks don't lie. They're in there some place right now, probably three days ahead of any of Townsend's troops. The only reason we got this close behind 'em is that we rode a train half the way."

Tom climbed down to examine the tracks.

"Looks like only three horses, and maybe three sets of moccasin tracks. That could mean only three Indians made it. They could be leading their horses, if they're too sore-footed to carry a rider."

Sam nodded, wondering if there were any casualties among Chama's men.

"Only way we're gonna find out is to track them down, Tom. A man could wander around in these canyons for months and never find them. Like you said, this is a hell of a waste of taxpayer money, but we've got our orders to help with this thing. I'd rather it was us who found 'em. That way, there's a chance we can talk them into giving up without a fight. Not much of a chance, mind you, but some. I've worn this badge a hell of a long time, and never refused to obey an order. Since this was a direct order from Fort Smith, I don't reckon I'll start now. I ain't never lied to Charlie, so I suppose we ought to start lookin' for these Comanches as hard as we can."

He touched a spur to the buckskin and rode into the wind, pulling his hat over his eyes to shield them from the dust blowing down the canyon. The wind carried a faint scent of rain, although there were no clouds on the horizon.

"Be damn glad you brought your slicker," Sam yelled above the wind. "When it rains in this country, it can float a boulder as big as a horse."

They rode up the canyon as dark fell. Sam followed the tracks until darkness hid them, feeling the throbbing pain grow worse in his right ankle. He dreaded the moment when nature forced him to climb down from his horse, for he knew what the pain would be like when he tried to stand on the bad ankle. He wondered idly if he could figure a way to relieve himself from the saddle, but the longer he thought about it, the more impossible it seemed.

A sudden gust of cold wind brought his thoughts to other things, as the smell of rain grew stronger. A hard rain would wash all the tracks of the Indians away. If a big rain came, there would be no tracks for them, or the troopers, to follow. Without tracks, the search for Chama would be hopeless, since the Palo Duro canyon ran for better than fifty miles west, and perhaps hundreds of miles in both directions in the offshoot canyons leaving the river. It had taken Mackenzie two months with twenty Apache scouts and two thousand troops to find the Kwahadies twenty years ago. Only a fool would keep looking with less than a hundred men, especially if a rain wiped out the trail they hoped to follow.

Sam lifted his face to the star-filled sky, grinning to

himself as he thought about a rain. Maybe Chama's medicine was mighty strong after all. Not only could he ride an impossible four hundred miles in six days, but it was beginning to look like the wise old fox could also make it rain when he needed it.

Several miles up the canyon, Sam heard the rumble of thunder overhead. A bank of clouds came from the northwest, covering the stars and the beginnings of a moon above the horizon, turning the floor of the canyon pitch-black.

"Best we find some high ground and take cover until morning," Sam yelled as the wind swept past them. "We could get washed plumb to the Gulf of Mexico, if it rains hard."

They untied their slickers and pulled them on. Then Sam rode to the edge of the river, scanning the dark cliffs on each side silently for a moment.

"We've got to gamble here," he said finally. "If it comes a big rain, we'll be trapped on one side or the other for a long time, until the river goes down. If Chama is on one side, and we're on the other, we might as well start back for Childress. My guess is, he rode up the southern bank to put the river between himself and Townsend's troops. Just another way of throwing everybody off, making us think he's headed for a hiding place on the south side of the canyon. We can't tell for sure in the dark, but I'd bet a new hat he's crossed to the north. Like I said, we'll have to gamble a little, but I'd bet I'm right."

Sam rode into the river, allowing the buckskin time to pick its way over the rocky riverbed until it reached the other side. Sam rode west again, looking for a trail leading to higher ground that would keep them from floodwaters if a heavy rain came. For several miles they rode along the steep cliff in total darkness, unable to find any passage out of the canyon. Lightning flashed overhead, followed by thunder that shook the ground under the horses' hooves.

It was pure chance, as they stopped to get their bearings, waiting for a flash of lightning to show them what lay ahead. When the lightning struck, Tom noticed a narrow slice in the limestone wall only a few yards away.

"This could be something," he said, climbing down to walk to the crevice.

When he touched the limbs partially covering the opening, he knew he had found the Comanches trail, for the limbs came from the crack too freely, piled in the opening to hide it from a casual eye.

"I think I found Chama's trail," Tom yelled above rattling thunder. "Come have a look."

Tom climbed up the slice. In another flash of lightning, at a turn in the passage, he found the hoof-prints of several ponies.

"I found tracks," he said, pulling the remainder of the brush from the opening. "It's gonna be a little tight in spots, but we can make it. If a man didn't know horses already made that climb, he'd never think to try it. Damn near straight up, Sam. Get a good hold on your saddlehorn."

Tom spurred his black gelding into the crevice. Shod hooves scrambled for footing, sending sparks into the dark in front of Sam, as Tom rode up to the first turn and went out of sight.

Sam tugged his hat a little lower and spurred into the opening. The buckskin clawed for footing, slipping to its knees, then up again to continue an almost perpendicular climb. The trail swung left, lessening the steep grade, the rock walls so close on either side that Sam could touch them with his hands.

For half an hour the horses struggled upward, turning often at sharp bends in the trail, while lightning flashed overhead, followed by rolling thunder. Finally, the path turned onto a flat depression in the rock, worn away by countless rains.

Tom had dismounted, and was walking toward a niche in the rock overlooking the yawning canyon.

"I saw something," Tom yelled above rattling thunder. "Looks like it could be a fresh grave."

With another flash of lightning, Sam saw the freshly dug mound of earth near the edge. He swung his throbbing leg over and stepped gingerly to the ground, feeling a jolt of fresh pain stab through his leg, as he tried to hobble behind Tom to the pile of dirt.

"It is a grave," Tom said softly. "One of the Comanches didn't make it."

Tom knelt and started wiping earth from the mound. Sam clamped his teeth together, hoping it would not be Chama lying under the shallow soil, but unable to look away as Tom uncovered the body.

Another flash of lightning revealed the Indian's face. Sam let out a sigh. The body was not Chama's. it was another of the old warriors he remembered, a man called Quahip, one of Chama's closest friends at Fort Sill.

"Been dead a long time," Sam said, smelling the putrid flesh. "They must have carried his body for several days, in order to bury him with his ancestors. Cover him up again, and let's keep movin'. I don't want to be caught in this place if a big rain hits. We'll be washed right off this cliff."

Sam limped back to his horse and took a big swallow of Tom's whiskey before he attempted the climb back into the saddle. The fluid in his ankle was the size of a melon. He would have to cut the boot off his foot if it got any worse.

Tom covered the body, swung up, then led the way to the other side of the pocket and continued to climb toward the top. Sam followed, cursing softly as he sipped whiskey, wishing this search for Chama could come to a speedy end, one way or the other.

A few minutes later Tom's gelding trotted out on a flat plateau, the top of the canyon stretching for many miles west. The first drops of rain began to fall as the fury of the storm grew, blowing into their faces as lightning struck around them.

"Better find cover pretty soon," Sam yelled, trotting his horse west into the wind.

They rode for half an hour into a driving rain. The wind whipped sheets of water into their faces, blinding them until a bolt of lightning brightened the sky. Before the light faded, Sam saw a shallow depression to their right, and a rocky overhang big enough for two men to wait out the storm.

Sam reined toward the basin and felt his horse slide down the trail to the bottom of slippery mud. At the rock ledge he halted his horse and stepped to the ground, rewarded for his effort by another sharp pain running up his leg.

He loosened the girth and let Tom fasten the hobbles on both mounts. Then he carried his bedroll up a slight incline to a dry spot beneath the overhang away from the rain, just as another torrent of rain pelted down into the basin.

Tom carried his bedroll and tossed it against the back of the shallow cave. A few sticks of dry wood lay at the base of the rock wall. Using fistfuls of dry grass and small sticks, he started a tiny fire in a circle of stones and poured water from his canteen into his coffeepot. After adding a few ground beans, in short order they smelled fresh coffee boiling while the storm raged in the skies overhead.

Sam leaned back against the rock and straightened his legs, feeling the fluid move in his ankle.

"Damn glad you brought this whiskey," he said, opening the pint again.

Tom built up the fire and removed two biscuits from Sam's oilskin. In a few minutes they sipped scalding hot coffee and ate Clara's biscuits and ham, watching a small river of water run past the sheltering cave. Their horses grazed a few yards away, hopping from one bunch of dry grass to the next in the driving rainstorm.

"Might as well take it easy, son," Sam said above the thunder. "From the looks of those clouds, we're gonna be here quite a spell."

Sam added whiskey to his coffee, then took off his hat to rest his head against the cool limestone. They finished their supper and let the fire die down to glowing embers, while the rain came down with a fury into the basin.

"This rain finishes our business here," Sam said after a long, thoughtful moment. "Won't be any tracks after a downpour like this. Come sunup, we'll have a looksee, but there won't be much we can do. With no trail to follow, Chama and his bunch will be too hard to

167

find. I ain't gonna spend my last three months as a U.S. Marshal wanderin' around this part of Texas. Charlie will understand. Once he knows the truth about all this, he'll agree we did the right thing comin' back."

Tom listened to the sounds of the rain a moment, thinking.

"We were pretty close behind them," he said finally. "That grave hadn't been dug more than a few hours. Could be they found shelter from this rain like us. Maybe in the morning, if we ride a few circles across this rim, we might find their tracks again in all this mud. It'll take a piece of luck, like finding that crack in the cliff, but we could try."

Sam clamped his jaw and said nothing. It was like Tom Ford, to see a thing all the way through. It was one of the reasons Sam had recommended him as his replacement in Cache, for Tom showed a special talent for seeing a job got done. This time, Sam found himself wishing Tom wasn't quite so dedicated to his badge, but Tom was right, of course. They should look tomorrow, to see if Chama waited out this rain someplace close by. If he knew Comanche habits at all, the Indians were long gone, pushing through the storm, knowing it would cover their tracks and putting as much distance as they could between themselves and whoever might follow. Unless Chama was too weakened to walk, he would surely have kept up his pace through the rain, certain that it would obliterate all signs of his passing.

"I suppose we could look around a little, if this rain lets up in the morning," Sam said before tossing down the last of his coffee. "We've come a long way and slept on mighty hard ground to go back empty-handed."

Tom gave Sam a knowing look across the embers. "Won't disappoint you any if we do, will it?"

Sam tried to keep the grin from his mouth.

"Not a damn bit, Deputy Ford. This is one time I won't be the least bit embarrassed to ride back with empty handcuffs."

10

Sergeant Hutto urged his horse through the mud. Rain pelted his hat brim and plastered his blue tunic to his skin. A bolt of lightning helped him find Captain Braverman in the dark, waiting beneath the sheltering limbs of a live oak tree. Before the lightning faded, Hutto saw the lines of soldiers huddled beside the river. Most of the men were off their horses, wearing slickers to keep out the driving rain. Hutto's disdain for rain gear set him apart from his men as he rejoined the waiting column to give his report. Not only had the captain donned his slicker first, before the order went down the line, he had also halted the column and ridden for the closest tree. Hutto shook his head as he reined over to Captain Braverman. The army wasn't a place for real men any longer. This detail would never catch up to the Indians, not in a thousand years.

"Rain's washed out everything, Cap'n," he said. "But I found one of their horses up yonder. A little pony from the post compound. Dead, with a bullet hole in its skull."

Braverman nodded. "Then we're on the right track, Sergeant. As soon as this rain lets up, we'll push on."

Hutto made a face, hidden by the darkness. "Might rain all night, Cap'n. We're losin' valuable time."

Braverman turned, glancing toward his men. Pools of watery mud encircled the line of troopers, glistening in a fading sheet of lightning overhead. "Those men aren't able to sustain a forced march, Sergeant. Not under these conditions. Send the order down to pitch tents. I want guards posted on the picket lines, just in case some of those Comanches try to slip back and steal some of our horses. If they've lost a horse, it means they're suffering the same as us. I have a feeling we're very close now. When the men are rested, we'll continue our pursuit. If some of the Comanches are walking, we'll catch up to them in short order. Perhaps tomorrow. Order the men to pitch tents, and remember to double the guard on our picket lines."

"Yessir," Hutto mumbled, reining his gelding away from the tree following a halfhearted salute. When he was out of earshot, he grumbled, "This is one hell of a way to chase Injuns. We couldn't catch up to a three-legged mule travelin' backwards at this rate. Might as well let the men off to pick daisies and write some letters home."

He found Corporal Storch seated on a rock, wrapped tightly in his slicker. "Break out the tents," Hutto snapped, dismounting. "Have Casey run a picket line. The captain says we'll wait until it stops raining. If you've got any knitting needles, you've got my permission to start on a pair of socks."

Hutto stormed down the line behind his corporal,

172

grumbling about the army while the order was shouted down the column. Mud sucked at the soldiers' boots as the formation was broken. Thunder rumbled across the skies.

"What about those Comanches?" Corporal Storch asked, taking Hutto's reins to picket his mount.

Hutto sighed. "They're likely plumb to California by now, Corporal. This outfit couldn't catch butterflies, much less a pack of Comanches."

A sheet of lightning revealed a further irritation. Some of the men had begun to erect their tents along the riverbank. If a big rain swelled the river out of its banks, the men would be swept downstream while they slept. "Damn fool green peas," he swore, shaking his head. "Hell, let 'em drown, for all I care." He stalked off toward the packhorses to find himself a tent.

Later, some of the men were able to get fires going in spots sheltered by stands of trees. Complaints about the rain and mud echoed through the dark, as soldiers tried to erect their small sleeping tents. Hutto watched the disarray with an overpowering sense of loss. Men crashed through the underbrush searching for dry firewood, making enough noise to wake the dead. Down in his gut, Hutto knew that if any of the Comanches had circled back to steal horses, they would have an easy time of it.

Captain Braverman found him, slogging through the deepening mud inspecting the bivouac, shrouded in his slicker. "There you are, Sergeant. Have the guards been posted?"

"I gave the order, sir. I was on my way to inspect the picket lines just now."

"Good. Can't be too careful. We may be surrounded by hostiles even now. Order the men to keep a sharp eye."

Hutto halted a wisecrack on the tip of his tongue, deciding it was a waste. Braverman wasn't any more capable of getting the job done right than his green troops. Rain pelted Hutto's slicker as he whirled away to inspect the picket line . . . he had donned the slicker as a concession to the times. Battle-hardened soldiers of Randy Hutto's era would have preferred walking naked down the aisle of church to being caught in a slicker during a summer rain. These kids at Fort Sill weren't real soldiers at all, not by old army standards.

Hutto left his tent to inspect the picket ropes, dreading what he would find. The storm raged above the encampment, sending a torrent down upon the sagging tents and waterlogged troopers. Sucking mud worsened the soldiers' plight, until hardly a place remained where deep boot prints did not exist. Rivulets of water swept through low spots, forming tiny rivers. The closer Hutto came to the picket line, the more certain he became of the ultimate doom of their mission. He wondered idly if Braverman's detail might become hopelessly stuck in this mud, unable to move when dawn came.

Blinded by a sheet of rain, he almost stumbled into the rump of a sorrel horse. The gelding jumped, as surprised as he, whirling to see him through the rain. Hutto cursed silently when he discovered the reason for the sorrel's presence in the middle of camp. Someone had forgotten to tie it properly to the picket rope, and now it wandered loose, trailing its halter shank.

"Might as well find those Comanches and make 'em

174

a present of half our horses," Hutto complained, leading the gelding toward the distant shapes of tethered horses south of the encampment. Sloshing through the mud, he passed a huddled sentry cradling a rifle.

"How'd this horse get loose, soldier?" Hutto snapped. "I found it wandering around the tents. How the hell are you gonna spot any Comanches slippin' up on us, if you can't even see a goddamn horse standing in plain sight?"

The sentry shook his head. Hutto saw the boy's face in a flicker of lightning. Rounded eyes were fearful when they beheld the sergeant's face. "I don't know, Sergeant. I been lookin' real close for them Injuns."

Hutto's shoulders slumped. A further discussion of the loose horse would be useless. He trudged past the sentry and led the horse to the picket rope.

"Who goes there?" someone shouted. "Identify yourself or I'll fire!"

Instinctively, Hutto ducked down behind the horses. "Don't shoot, soldier!" he cried.

Well past midnight, there was a strange sound, like thunder, only different in a vague way. Hutto sat up in his tent and rubbed sleep from his eyes, straining to hear the roar above the patter of raindrops on the tent. It was unmistakably a foreign noise, and not the natural rumble of distant thunder.

He pulled on his boots and slicker before crawling out of the tent. Sheets of rain swirled around him. Below the crest of the knoll where his tent stood, the sound grew louder, and then he knew its source.

"Pull out for high ground!" he shouted, cupping his hands to his mouth. "The river's rising!"

Upstream, the river was roaring. Hutto knew from experience that time was precious before a wall of water swept over the camp, taking everything in its path along with it. Puddled rainwater squished away from his boots as he started running between the tents, shouting a warning.

A bolt of lightning coursed across the inky sky, brightening the riverbank. Hutto saw muddy water churning past the river's edge, carrying uprooted trees like matchsticks, tossing trunks and limbs about in swirling eddies encircled by frothy foam. The rain-swollen Red was barely the width of a man's hand from leaving its banks. "Run for high ground!" Hutto shouted, trotting through the sucking mud as rapidly as he could.

He saw frightened horses fighting the picket ropes downstream, and he knew that unless he could reach them quickly, the rising river would drown them. Yet the same fate awaited the men, should any of them fail to heed his cries. Shoulders hunched against the wind-driven rain, he trotted faster, yelling into the tents at the top of his voice.

Soon soldiers were swarming along the soggy river-bank mud, trying to pull their gear toward safety. Between flashes of lightning, men were bumping into each other, blinded by the dark and the heavy rain. Some stumbled and fell in the mud, only to be overrun by fleeing men behind. The scene was utter confusion, and Hutto knew the horses still faced peril, unless he could reach them before the flash flood got there first.

A shouting trooper ran into Hutto in the dark.

"Come with me," he cried, trying to be heard above the roaring wall of water. "We've got to cut those horses off the ropes before they drown!"

Somewhere upstream, a tree limb cracked. Seconds later, Hutto was swept off his feet by a force so powerful that he could only brace his fall with his elbows. He fell on his back, splashing into a foot or more of churning foam. The trooper behind him cried out, kicking and splashing as the water carried him past. Hutto grabbed the soldier's slicker and held on until he regained his footing, helping the boy to his feet. "Keep moving!" Hutto shouted above the storm. "We've got to get to those horses!"

Slogging through chunks of driftwood and broken limbs, Hutto and the trooper made their way to one end of a picket rope. The sergeant fumbled for his knife and cut the rope, freeing dozens of terrified horses that were snorting and fighting the rope's pull.

Farther downstream, Hutto glimpsed a sentry struggling to unfasten a second picket line. Bolting horses jerked the rope from the soldier's hands, worsening the sentry's plight. Hutto tried to run forward to help with the rope, and promptly fell flat in knee-deep water. When he tried to rise, he was swept off his feet again, this time knocked backward when his boots were torn from underneath him. Fighting the current, he pawed his way downstream, using his hands until his foot caught on something solid. When he stood, the water was waist-deep around him. Stumbling along with the water's pull, he saw the picket rope snap a few yards to his right. Thrashing hooves and frightened nickering marked the spot where the freed horses tried to escape the river toward higher ground. Fearing for his own life now, Hutto turned and grabbed a swaying tree branch, pulling his way behind the lunging horses to solid footing. Gasping for air, he staggered uphill.

A line of troopers huddled on a rainswept ridge above the river, watching the power of the flash flood roar past. In brief flashes of lightning, Hutto could see dozens of loose horses running away from the river. Trudging down the line of men, he wondered how many lives had been lost to the sudden flood. All their supplies would be gone, and the saddles and bridles. From the beginning, he had known this campaign bore the earmarks of a disaster. Led by an incompetent, unfieldworthy commander who sought personal gain, the detail from Fort Sill would be a military laughing-stock when the report reached higher-ups. Braverman would be lucky to avoid a court-martial, if any men lost their lives. At best, he would be assigned to some remote supply depot in the wilderness until the end of his military career, probably along with the men who served directly under him. Searching the faces down the line for the captain, Hutto wondered what the Arizona desert would be like in July. Would it be any worse than Fort Sill?

He found Captain Braverman shivering inside his slicker. The captain's face was ashen, and for a time he seemed not to recognize Sergeant Hutto when the sergeant spoke. "Have you taken a roll, Captain, to see how many men are not accounted for?" Hutto asked.

Braverman blinked. "No, Sergeant," he said quietly. "Assemble the men and let's see who's missing. Good thinking, Hutto. And perhaps we should send some men to round up our horses."

178

The sergeant's jaw tightened, then relaxed. "Yes sir. I'll see to it, when the men are counted. We've lost our supplies and probably most of the saddles. Likely a few horses, too. If you'll pardon me for making the observation, Cap'n, I think we're in a hell of a shape to continue."

Braverman stiffened. "Nonsense, Sergeant. At first light we'll take stock of our situation. Regardless of our losses, we will stay hard on the tracks of those Comanches."

Hutto shook his head. "There won't be any tracks, Cap'n. This rain will wash out everything."

Braverman aimed an angry look toward Hutto. "That would be a command decision, Sergeant, and in case you've forgotten, I am the commanding officer here. We will resume our pursuit of those Indians at first light. Take a few men downstream to round up what horses you can, as soon as you've conducted a roll call. I will order the rest to scour the riverbank for whatever gear we can salvage. That's all, Sergeant."

Hutto saluted and trudged off into the rain, grinding his teeth in frustration. He picked two men from the end of the line and gave the order to assemble along the ridge. Thunder rumbled above the sounds of the raging river, while the troopers formed a roll call. The Troop's Roll was forever lost to the river in Hutto's gear, however he knew most of the names by heart anyway, and a gap in the assembly would tell him who was missing.

Remarkably, every man stood accounted for when Hutto walked down the line. He tapped three men on the shoulder and formed a detail to go after the horses, leading them off into a driving wind that pelted their faces with raindrops. Water squished around in his boots, adding to his misery as he led his men away from the river.

Mounted on the gentlest animals they could find, Hutto rode at the front of his soggy procession leading strays. The storm had not lessened, and only luck brought them upon loose horses in sheltering stands of trees south of the riverbank. A few grazed on short grass in spite of the weather, horses starved by the continued forced march behind the Comanches. Behind Hutto, a trooper's teeth chattered. Waterlogged clothing added a touch of ice to the wind as it swirled around them.

Hours later, Hutto turned to count the horses. Twenty-six animals plodded along behind the detail, tied together head-and-tail. Riding bareback, without the control of bridles, their progress had been painfully slow. Pushing farther south, Hutto led his shivering party through the rain, wondering how bad things could be at Fort Grant, Arizona. At least it wouldn't rain.

By Hutto's reckoning, this had been the longest night of his life, and when he pulled his pocket watch to check the time in a glimmer of lightning, he discovered the night was far from ending. "Almost three," he grumbled. Better than two hours of darkness remained before dawn. The storm showed no signs of abating. He turned to Corporal Storch, facing the horizontal rain driven by blasts of wind. "Let's keep looking for horses!" he shouted.

They rode over a rise just south of the river to find an

180

unexpected sight. On a flat plain below the turbulent floodwaters, dark shapes were huddled around a pair of automobiles. Two dim kerosene headlamps gleamed through the pelting rain. Hutto could make out the shapes of men near the cars.

"They're stuck in the mud again, Sergeant," Corporal Storch remarked. "Looks like they're trying to pull one out with the other. I never figured they'd get those buggies out of the river, but it appears they unstuck a couple of them."

Hutto scowled. The posse from Mangum under Sheriff Dobbs had somehow proceeded along the river in a pair of automobiles. "Wonder where they found enough gasoline to get so far," he said. "Let's ride down for a closer look."

"We're liable to get shot," the corporal warned. "Remember they was all carryin' guns, and it's mighty damn dark out here. They might figure us for Injuns and open fire."

Storch had somehow grasped a truth which had escaped Hutto, not the sort of clearheaded thinking Corporal Storch was known for. "We can identify ourselves from a distance," Hutto said. "We'll have the wind at our backs, so our voices will carry. Hang on to those horses, men. Whatever you do, don't let go of those ropes."

Hutto urged his sorrel off the rise, vaguely concerned that Storch could be right about the posse taking shots at them. "Hey there!" Hutto began at the top of his lungs. "United States Cavalry under Captain Lloyd Braverman! We're riding in, so hold your fire!"

A lantern flickered, held aloft by one of the possemen. Men in yellow oilskins peered into the dark.

181

"Who goes there?" someone cried.

"Sergeant Hutto. Third U.S. Cavalry from Fort Sill. We saw your headlamps from the hill."

A few possemen lowered the rifles in their hands. Hutto recognized Sheriff Dobbs in the lantern's glow. Leading their horses, Hutto rode up to the first automobile and sawed back on the halter rope.

Sheriff Dobbs's hat brim drooped in the pouring rain. He took a step closer to the mounted soldiers. "It would appear we're destined to pass each other in the mud from time to time, sonny," he barked. "Got the damn things stuck again, as you can see. Now this time, I won't listen to any refusal to lend us a hand with these horseless carriages. We need some assistance here, and a team of those horses will do nicely."

Hutto shook his head. "No saddles, Sheriff. No way to tie horses to those bumpers. We lost our horses when that river sent a flash flood down. Saddles and gear to boot. There's nothing we can do to help right now. I'm under orders to round up our horses and get back to camp, so we can proceed at first light."

"Did you say somethin' about loose horses?" someone asked from the body of possemen.

Hutto shook his head. "Lost 'em all to that wall of floodwater around midnight. We're gathering them up, the ones we can find."

"Maybe them wasn't Apaches after all," someone else muttered. It was hard to hear the remark in the rain.

"You saw the Injuns?" Hutto asked.

"Thought we did," Sheriff Dobbs replied. "Fired a few shots when they galloped over that ridge. Too dark to see, but we could hear their horses. Jim Bob swore he

182

got a glimpse of 'em when lightning struck."

"It was Apaches, all right," a tall fellow explained, looking at the men around him. "They was layin' flat on their horses, like Apaches always do. I seen one plain as day, a'fore the sky went black."

Hutto wondered what the odds were against the Fort Sill Comanches circling back. The Indians had maintained a southwest course since they left the reservation, and it made no sense that any of the bunch would double back ... unless Captain Braverman had been right when he guessed the runaways might make a try at stealing a few of the cavalry horses. "I doubt you saw our Injuns," Hutto remarked. "It's more likely that you saw some of the horses we lost when that flood broke our picket ropes."

"I seen one plain as day," the man repeated, with less certainty now.

Hutto surveyed the stranded cars. "Where'd you get the gasoline to come so far?" he asked.

"We brung extra cans along," Sheriff Dobbs explained. "I ain't some tinhorn when it comes to chasin' wanted men. We outfitted ourselves proper before we left. Hadn't been for this goddamn rain and that riverbottom, we'd have already put them Apaches in irons by now. Bad luck, is all it was, that kept us from catchin' up to them renegades. Now climb down off that horse, sonny, and lend us a hand. We can tie some ropes around the horses' necks, and we'll be out of this mud in a jiffy."

"I've got my orders," Hutto replied. "Sorry, Sheriff, but I'm afraid I'll have to deny your request."

Sheriff Dobbs whipped open his coat, pulling his revolver. "Like hell you will," he snapped. "I'm a duly sworn peace officer, and I'm within my legal rights to seize property, when I need it to apprehend escaped criminals. Get down off that horse, soldier, and make it snappy. I'll use this gun, if you force my hand on it."

Some of the rifles in the hands of the possemen appeared, aimed at Hutto and his men. Rankled at being taken by surprise, Hutto started to complain. "We're United States Army. You can't seize government property, and that's what these horses happen to be. You could be sent to federal prison for this, Sheriff. Think it over, before you go too far."

"I've already thought it over. Get down off that damn horse or I'll shoot you off of it. Understand?"

Hutto took a deep breath. "Captain Braverman won't stand for this. He'll file charges with the federal marshal."

Sheriff Dobbs seemed unconcerned. "Don't give a damn just now, sonny. It's pouring rain and these carriages are stuck, so I'm taking official action here. Slide off them horses, or you'll need one of them army doctors to patch you up."

Hutto sighed and gave the order to dismount.

"We'll only need two," Sheriff Dobbs added. "Just long enough to get these contraptions out of the mud to higher ground. Boys, harness up two of those horses with whatever you can find. We're wasting valuable time with all this palaver."

Several possemen took Hutto's sorrel and a second gelding, leading them to a place in front of the pale headlamps. Hutto stood back to watch the proceedings. Corporal Storch and the other troopers followed the sergeant out of harm's way.

Tying pieces of rope together, crude loops were

fashioned to the horses and then to the front bumper of the automobile. Men shouted instructions that no one else seemed inclined to follow, until a posseman took the steering wheel in the first car while another turned the crank. Seconds later, a motor sputtered to life, spooking the horses into their ropes. More possemen found places to push against the frame. Tires threw mud as wheels began to spin. A posseman near one rear wheel slipped and fell to his knees, showered by splattering mud as the sounds of the motor grew louder. A yoke around one horse's neck snapped and suddenly the gelding broke free, spooked by the roaring engine. Sheriff Dobbs was barking orders to his men, pointing this way and that with the barrel of his pistol. Someone tried to cling to the rope halter on the escaping gelding, being dragged through the mud until he was out of sight in the dark, yelling, "Whoa, whoa you sonofabitch."

"Damn," Hutto hissed, clamping his jaw. He'd spent nineteen years in the military, and couldn't remember such a seemingly unending string of disasters. From the moment they left Fort Sill, it appeared nothing was meant to go right. He whirled around to Corporal Storch. "Get over there and lend those fools a hand. Otherwise, we'll be here 'til noon."

Hutto held the leadropes on the remaining captured horses, while his corporal and the pair of troopers walked over to the stranded automobile leading a gentle brown gelding. Sheriff Dobbs halted the driver long enough for the soldiers to tie the horse to the bumper, then the effort was resumed again.

Slowly, barely an inch at a time, the car was lifted out of the deep ruts, freed from its muddy moorings.

Turning uphill when the horses were untied, the driver aimed the sputtering machine toward a slab of rock. Amid cheers from some of the possemen, the conveyance reached the rocky knob.

A similar operation unstuck the second car. When both automobiles rested on the hilltop, the horses were returned to Hutto's men. Sheriff Dobbs came over, his gun holstered now, slipping once as he crossed watery automobile tracks.

"You can have your horses back, sonny," he said, sleeving mud from his face. "I've been thinkin' . . . we ought to work together on this thing. Ride back and tell your captain that I'd like a word with him. We'll be along before morning, stayin' on these bluffs so the damn carriages don't get stuck again. Tell your captain to ride over and we'll discuss this thing. Dodson has put up a reward for the capture of those Apaches, and some of my boys feel they're entitled to it. We've come a hell of a long way, and we've been through a bunch of hardship to get here. If that captain will just be reasonable, we can work together on this Indian affair."

Hutto swung up on the sorrel's back, biting his tongue to keep a string of cusswords inside his mouth. "You stuck a gun in my face, and now you want us to work together, Sheriff?"

The sheriff stiffened. "I took official action. You was gonna leave us there, stuck like we was, and I'm carryin' legal warrants in my coat pocket for ol' Geronimo and his bunch. It don't appear you know much about the law, soldier. I've been a peace officer for thirty-four years . . . started out back when there was murderin' redskins behind every tree around

186

Mangum, before much of the Territory even got settled. Started out as constable over in the Nations, back when Belle Starr an' Henry run a gang all over . . ."

Before the sheriff was finished, Hutto wheeled his mount and rode away from the discussion, leading his men and the string of horses.

"Hey!" Sheriff Dobbs cried, "don't forget to tell that captain of yours that I want a word with him. We'll be comin' along shortly."

A clap of thunder rolled across the sky. Hutto ignored the sheriff's remark, swinging west of the river to look for more strays. To the east, a faint graying had begun along the horizon, but when he checked his pocket watch under the next lightning flash, the time was still only a few minutes after five.

Hunched into the wind, they started combing thickets of live oak and mesquite for more horses. Just once, Hutto wondered if the posse might have seen and fired at galloping Comanches in the dark. As unlikely as it seemed, the possibility made him more watchful when he entered dark groves of trees, nagged by the thought that his pistol belt and rifle had washed downstream with his tent when the floodwaters came.

11

Windblown sheets of rain poured down on Chama as he felt his way along *Habbe Pia*. Lightning flashed overhead, followed by thunder that shook the ground under his feet. Chama pulled his pony behind him along the narrow path, surrounded by walls of rock that seemed to touch the stormy sky. They were moving deeper into the limestone cliff, a slow drop below the canyon rim on the old warrior's path leading to Pena Pah. His pony limped with each step, lifting its head and shoulders to avoid the sharp stones at the bottom of the path, pulling Chama backward with the pull on the jaw rein when the pony tried to stop. The rain came so hard, he could not see the others behind him, until a flash of lightning lighted the skies above the crevice, just long enough for him to see Conas atop his pony, slumped forward in pain, trying to cling to the mane as Taoyo held him on the pony's back. Chama's feet had no feeling, numbed by the rocks and mud washing down the bottom of the trail. He knew he was staggering with each step, and felt as if he would

189

fall at any moment, were it not for the pull of the rein over his shoulder. The storm came down with the fury of a cougar, roaring and pelting water down his back, soaking his shirt and leggings, making each step more difficult as the weight of his clothing almost pulled him to the ground. His moccasins sloshed through the sticky mud, pulling at his feet, wearing away what little strength he had left. But the walls of *Habbe Pia,* the Arrow Path, were familiar now. In the flashes of lightning, he saw etchings made by The People, a collection of pictures drawn to show brave deeds in battle and hunting parties killing the buffalo. They were very close to the hidden canyon. Chama forced his legs to continue, in spite of the mud tugging at his feet and the weight of his water-soaked clothing. The rock drawings spoke to him, telling of the end of his journey.

His foot caught against a rock, and he fell forward on his face, sprawling in the mud when he let go of the pony's rein. He tried to push himself up on his hands, but the pelting rain drove him back in the mud.

He felt the pony nuzzle his face, snorting softly. With all his strength he pushed up again, drawing his knees under him. A hand caught his arm and helped him to his feet. Taoyo stood in the downpour, steadying Chama, a look of fear in his eyes.

"I thought I heard a *Tosi Tivo* bullet," the boy cried above the wind, "and I saw you fall. But it was only the thunder."

Chama clung to the boy's shoulder, gasping for breath.

"We are very close to Pena Pah. Have Poke stay with Conas and help him ride the pony. You must walk with

190

me, Taoyo, and help me take the last steps to the canyon."

Taoyo put a shoulder under Chama's arm, then he picked up the trailing jaw rein and started down the path, staggering under the weight. For a distance they moved slowly, slipping in the mud as the trail dropped lower into the rock.

Suddenly the trail dropped sharply, and as they walked, the rock walls on each side widened, then disappeared in the darkness. They stopped, waiting for the next flash of lightning, but Chama did not need the light to know he was standing in the entrance to Pena Pah, for his heart spoke to him, telling him the journey was over at last. He had come back to the place of his birth. His spirit felt the peace of the canyon before his eyes revealed it in the next bolt of lightning.

The sky brightened as a clap of thunder shook the ground. Below the spot where they stood, a giant fissure in solid limestone yawned for half a mile in front of them, an irregular slice carved out of the plateau north of *Pahehona* where the hand of Powva had lifted a giant piece from the crust of mother earth. As the light faded, Chama saw the groves of trees scattered thickly over the canyon floor, and the reflection of the stream winding through the middle of Pena Pah, as it snaked its way from one end of the valley to the other. A deer lifted its head near the stream, grass dangling from its mouth as it watched curiously, examining the strange two-legged creatures on the trail above the canyon. Pena Pah was just as Chama remembered it, running from east to west as a deep cut in the limestone mountain.

Chama sank to his knees in the mud, as rain pelted down on his uplifted face. He lifted his arms to the sky and began a chant, his voice shaking. Rain poured into his mouth, driven by the wind, pounding against his cheeks as the words came from his mouth. He could feel tears in his eyes, washed away quickly by the rain until his prayer was finished.

Poke came up beside Taoyo, slipping in the mud, his eyes fixed on the canyon.

"We have come home, Chama," he said above the wind. "With the strength of Quinne, you have shown us the way. When all the Sata Exiponi surrendered their spirits to the *Tosi Tivo*, there was one among us who would not give up hope. One last warrior still fought the blue coats with his spirit. Even with all the soldiers at Fort Sill, they could not defeat you, Chama. We are free again, to follow the great chief of the Sata Exiponi. Lead the way down, Chief Toyah Chama."

Chama struggled to his feet. He turned to his warriors, then he started down the slope leading to the canyon floor as a bolt of lightning lit the sky.

They reached level ground, standing in knee-deep meadow grass at the edge of a grove of live oak. Chama led the way under the sheltering limbs as water poured into the canyon. All four fell on the grass, exhausted. The ponies wandered away, grazing hungrily on the lush grasses, while the four Comanches dropped off in a deep, dreamless sleep, with the soft music of the rain-drops pattering down on the leaves above them.

His eyes came open when Taoyo touched his shoulder. The boy pointed to three wild turkey hens in a clearing beyond the trees. The rain had ended during the night, and as the first rays of light came over the canyon rim, Chama looked at the hens, then at the tree-studded valley glistening with the recent rainfall.

Chama came tiredly to his knees. Taoyo handed him his bow and one arrow. Chama fitted the notch to the gutstring and drew back, sending an arrow into the closest turkey hen as the others flapped their wings away from the clearing.

Taoyo helped Chama to his feet, grinning before he walked to the clearing to pick up the hen.

"I can build a small fire under the trees so the smoke will not be seen by the soldiers," he said proudly. "Poke showed me how to build the fire so the limbs will keep the smoke from rising in the sky."

Chama looked at the boy silently for a moment, remembering his worries over taking Taoyo with him to Palo Duro. The boy had become a warrior on their journey. In only a few days he had taken the responsibilities of manhood on his shoulders. Without him, they could not have made it over the fences, or kept Conas on his pony.

"You will cook the hen, Taoyo. But first, I must keep the promise I made to your grandfather. Follow me."

At first, Taoyo's eyes were troubled, for he did not understand why Chama was leading him toward the other end of Pena Pah. He followed Chama beside the stream, clearly puzzled by their walk, until they came to a pool at the western wall of the canyon.

Chama walked to the edge of the pool and lay down on his stomach. The water was clear, in spite of the rain, revealing colorful stones along the bottom. A fish

193

darted away from Chama's shadow as he held his lips to the glassy surface and took a mouthful of cool water. He swallowed, remembering. For a big part of his lifetime, he had come here to drink from the spring, until the Comanches left Pena Pah as prisoners of the *Tosi Tivo*. For most of his eighteen taums of imprisonment, he had dreamed of this pool. It was this dream, and dreams of the canyon, which brought him to the bluff to pray for freedom from the reservation. Those dreams had given him hope, the memories of clear, sweet water in Pena Pah. Without this memory, he would surely have become like the others, waiting only for death with no hope of returning to this place. After so long, and so many dreams, he was at last tasting the cool water again.

He gazed down at his reflection on the surface. Once, his reflection had been no different than Taoyo's, a young warrior come to drink his fill before leaving to hunt buffalo. His reflection now was very different, a wrinkled face and braids of gray-white hair, an old man come to take a last drink from the spring before the spirit journey. So many taums had passed, and with them, an end to the five Comanche tribes as a free people. So much had changed since he last drank water in Pena Pah.

He turned on his side and spoke to the boy.

"Lie down. Drink from the pool. I gave my promise to your grandfather that I would show you this place, and let you taste the cool water. This is what so many of our people gave their lives for, this canyon, this water. Pena Pah is filled with the spirits of brave Comanches who have died, defending our homes from the soldiers."

Taoyo went to his stomach and put his lips to the surface.

"The water is sweet, Taoyo, like honey. But our freedom, to come to the pool and drink whenever we want, is the sweetest taste of all."

Chama came to his feet and looked around him. In the early light the beauty of the canyon seemed magnified, the deep green forests and the wandering course of the tiny stream. The happy sounds of water gurgling over the rocks where the stream left the pool filled the silence. Chama walked through the stream toward the south wall of the canyon, remembering the meadow where the Kwahadie buffalo lodges stood. Taoyo walked beside him through deep grass, startling quail and bluejays, feeling the dew soak his grandfather's moccasins as they walked among the trees. A deer jumped from a patch of shade, bounding off toward the stream.

"The doe is fat," Chama whispered, unwilling to break the silence with his voice. "We will have food for the winter. The Pena Pah has waited for us, keeping the animals well fed for the day the Comanches returned."

They entered a broad meadow, and at once, Chama was overcome with a feeling of sadness. A few of the buffalo hide conics still stood after eighteen taums, the lodgepoles naked and scorched from the fire set by Mackenzie's soldiers. He and the boy walked among the remains of the Kwahadie village, passing blackened humps of charred buffalo hide, still visible under thick grass and brush. Several of the old firepits still held ashes, as if the fires burned only yesterday. Chama knew he would find the bones of many of his people in the underbrush and beneath the charred remains of the lodges. So many died here, fighting the soldiers who fired down on the village from the rim above Pena Pah. It had been the blackest day in all Comanche history, as the Kwahadie women and children were slaughtered by unending volleys of gunfire. Three of Chama's wives died around him, reloading his guns, struck down by the hail of bullets from above. Somewhere in the village, three women died bravely near the spot where Chama drove his *Ma-wea* in the ground, to fight in the spot until death came, or until he tasted victory. Only when Buffalo Hump signaled a stop to the fighting did he put down his rifles, standing among his fallen wives in a pool of Kwahadie blood.

He shook away the memory and walked through the village with the sweet smells of the canyon in his nose. There was no smell of burned gunpowder, or the coppery smell of blood. The cries of the dying women and children were gone, replaced by a silence so deep he could hear his moccasins whispering through the wet grass.

"Was this our village?" Taoyo asked softly, gazing at the ruins of more than a dozen conics in the meadow.

"It was once a happy place, the air filled with the sounds of laughing children and the smells of buffalo meat cooking over the firepits. In a canyon to the north we kept more than six hundred ponies. The People had no fear in this place, for there was no tribe on mother earth strong enough to make war on the Comanches. Then the soldiers came, so many they hid the sun when they attacked us from the canyon rim. Our people were taken by surprise. No one could believe an enemy would come to Pena Pah to make war. In all our history, no one came to Palo Duro to fight us."

196

Taoyo swept the canyon rim with his eyes, his face clouded.

"The soldiers may come again, Chama. We must not let them take us by surprise again. We must always be ready, and keep a watch on the trail to the canyon."

Chama turned to the boy and placed a hand on his left shoulder, a traditional greeting among Comanches, given only to a warrior who had proven himself in battle.

"Spoken like a true warrior, Taoyo. With your sharp eyes and ears, no enemy will ever slip up on us here. From this day, you will no longer carry the name of a boy. It is time to call you by the warrior's name given to you by your father—Pemero Okoma. From this day, until no Comanches make this canyon home, you are called Yellow Bull."

The boy stood proudly, until Chama took his hand from his shoulder.

"Walk with me, Okoma, to our camp and prepare the turkey for the other warriors, for I am hungry."

They walked side by side beneath the glistening trees, until they reached the grove where Conas and Poke slept. Poke awakened as they approached, lifting on one arm as the boy gathered dry leaves and sticks to build a fire.

Using flint rocks, they built a fire and cleaned the hen. Conas awoke to the smells of roasting meat, a grin spreading over his wrinkled face as he came to sit by the fire.

"Once, when my eyes first opened, I thought I was still in a dream," he said, looking around him at the beauty of the valley. "But I see it is not a dream. We have come home. In all my years on mother earth, this

197

is the happiest day of my life."

Poke came to his feet and shouldered his Spencer, throwing a look over his shoulder to the mouth of the canyon.

"It is true, Conas, this is a happy time. We must not allow happiness to make us careless. We must be ready to fight, if they find our tracks in the canyon."

Chama left the trees to stand in the sunlight, watching the rim around Pena Pah. Then he came to the fire and took a piece of roasted turkey and his rifle.

"I will go back to *Habbe Pia* and watch for the soldiers," he said softly. "Rest, and walk through the canyon. I will come back when I see no soldiers have found the secret paths."

Sam hobbled to his horse, casting a look toward the blue skies and puffy white clouds to the west.

"No more rain," he said, as he tied his bedroll behind his saddle. "Unless we find some tracks to follow, we'll have clear weather for the ride back to Childress."

Tom swung aboard his black, scanning the western horizon.

"Let's have a look around for a spell, just in case they waited out the storm last night."

They rode west, staying within sight of the canyon rim, trotting their horses across slabs of solid rock. Years back, Sam had come to this part of Texas after an outlaw gang, and many years earlier, to make a trade with Quannah Parker for a white captive girl. The last time he saw Palo Duro, he joined up with marshals from Sweetwater to track down the gang led by a quick-handed gunfighter named Billy Blue.

The marshals tracked Blue and his gang to a canyon in the western edge of Palo Duro, and made a short fight out of his arrest. But Blue was a white man and not a Comanche, leaving a plain trail through the maze of canyons. It was another matter entirely to track Comanches in this rock. The best of the trackers with Mackenzie had taken months to pick up Indian sign. Sam knew there was little chance they would find Chama's tracks on this plateau, but it was a part of Tom Ford's temperament to try like hell at any task, thus there was nothing to do but ride until sundown and make the effort.

They rode into a wide basin and drew rein. Three trails left the spot in three different directions. They trotted over to each passage and swept the ground for sign, but with last night's heavy rain, they found only mud and rock.

"Let's split up," Tom said thoughtfully, gazing at the three choices.

Sam looked up the trail leading almost due west, and gave a nod of agreement.

"I'll ride this one out for a few hours. You choose one of the others. We'll meet back here an hour before dark."

Tom reined away to trot into one of the fissures. Before Tom was out of sight, Sam spurred his horse into the beginnings of another steep-walled crevice and began a plodding walk between the walls of stone.

In less than half an hour he opened the whiskey and drank a mouthful, already nagged by the pain in his swollen ankle, even though it was early in the day. The action of his horse sent a sharp pain up his leg, even at a walk. Sam thought quickly that there was too little whiskey, in light of the long ride back to Childress that he faced. All night he tried to escape the pain, but because of the swelling he could not remove the boot to rub some of the salve on his ankle. Whiskey was the only remedy, and it was in short supply in Palo Duro.

He wound along the passage for several hours, looking for the tracks of ponies, silently hoping he would find none in the mud, and, too, hoping Tom would fare no better. While he rode he drank steadily from the pint, until the last precious swallows loomed at the bottom as his last means of escape from the pain in his foot. For a time he entertained himself with the wishful notion that Tom had another bottle hidden in his saddlebags, but he knew it was only wishful thinking. There was no more whiskey, only a long hot ride back to Childress with an ankle the size of a cantaloupe.

He knew this would be his last ride on a horse for any distance. His joints simply would not allow it any more, another sign of rapidly advancing old age and uselessness. His body refused to cooperate any longer, protesting too much with the jolt from a horse's gait, allowing him no pleasure as a horseman. He was doomed to the seat of his Star touring car for the rest of his days, a gloomy thought for a man who loved horses. He found himself wondering again how Chama, well past Sam in years, could manage a four-hundred-mile ride . . . and without a saddle. Only a man who had ridden behind him on a horse could begin to understand the magnitude of such a feat. Sam had ridden only half the distance, and every bone in his body screamed for an end to the ride.

He drank the last swallow of whiskey and tossed the

bottle away when the sun sat directly overhead. He decided to ride another hour before he started back, feeling some pleasure at the fact that he had found no pony tracks.

The trail narrowed abruptly, the rock walls so close he had trouble pushing the gelding through without bumping his injured foot. A half-mile farther, he decided he had come far enough and began looking for a place wide enough to turn his gelding around.

He squeezed through another quarter-mile of passageway, unable to find a place to change directions. Forced to continue, he listened to the buckskin's hooves clatter over the rocky bottom, echoing in the distance as the trail dropped lower in the limestone mountain.

Suddenly the buckskin snorted and tried to rear up on its hind legs, frightened by something ahead, its ears cocked forward. Sam gripped the saddlehorn and fought to stay in the saddle, as he tried to look past his horse's ears to see what had startled the animal. Sam pulled the reins to steady himself, just as a figure leapt in front of his horse a few yards away.

Sam blinked, taken by complete surprise. Standing in the middle of the pathway was old Chama, with a rifle leveled at Sam's chest, a fire burning in the old man's eyes as he crouched, the gun ready to fire.

Sam knew at once the old warrior meant to kill him. The look on Chama's face left little doubt of his intentions.

Sam lifted both palms, to show he carried no weapon, and waited.

"Why did they send you, Man-Who-Wears-The-Star?"

Sam observed Chama's broad stance, ready to bear the kick of his rifle. His hands were steady as he swung the barrel toward Sam's face.

"I came for a talk," Sam said, as his horse settled beneath him. "Before you kill me, I will tell you what is in my heart. Kill me, but let me speak first."

As he looked into his fiery black eyes, he was certain Chama would not listen to talk of surrender. Chama had led his men across four hundred dangerous miles to reach this destination. One look at his face was enough. He would not go back to Fort Sill, no matter what words Sam said to him.

"Speak quickly," Chama said, lowering the rifle a few inches. "I will listen. Of all the *Tosi Tivo* I have known, you are the only one I have no wish to kill. Why did they send you?"

Sam lowered his hands, knowing whatever he said would have to be pretty good if he intended to stay alive.

"I did not want to come, Chama. My chief sent me. It is my job to try to talk you into going back to Fort Sill. I have no choice but to say the words from my chief."

Chama lifted the rifle again, his face drawn into a snarl.

"I choose death over the reservation. I will not go back. I will die from a soldier's bullet, but I will not go back with you."

Sam sighed, for he was not wrestling with his conscience any longer. He knew he could never attempt bringing Chama and the others back against their wishes. If Chama let him live, he would ride back to Fort Sill without any further effort to arrest the Comanches.

"I know why you ran away from the fort, Chama. Fort Sill is no place for any man. It is a sad thing to look at the Comanches the way they are now. For many years I could not see what was happening to your people. I chose not to look, for I am a white man, and the Indians are commanded to stay on the reservation by white man's law. But it is wrong to keep another human being in such a way. Men are not animals. The law of my people is not a just law, to force all Indians to live together in such a small place, guarded by soldiers. I speak truth when I say I am glad you made your escape to Palo Duro. I did not bring the soldiers with me. They are many days to the east, still trying to catch up with you. I don't know how you did it, but you put many suns between yourselves and the soldiers. Maybe you can live the rest of your lives here, if you hide your tracks carefully. My heart is glad for you. I speak truth. *Suvate.*"

Chama stood silently for a long time, reading Sam's face, piercing him with a look. Sam looked back over his shoulder at the pathway he had followed, and spoke again.

"The choice is yours, Chama. If you let me live, I will ride back and tell the soldiers I could not find your tracks. Like you, Chama, I am at the end of my road through life. I have grown too old to do the job of a marshal. My bones ache, and I can no longer sit my horse without pain. It is my wish to die where I am happy, at my lodge with my wife. She will care for me when I am too old or too sick to climb from my bed If you choose to let me live, I will ride back and tell my chief I am too old and tired to spend my last days looking for the tracks of a few Comanches. Let us have peace between us, old warrior. I will not show the soldiers your tracks. Let the rains and the winds wipe the prints of your ponies from the face of the earth forever. I give you my word I will not show the soldiers to this place."

Chama was silent, but Sam was certain the fire was gone from his eyes. In a moment Chama lowered the barrel of his rifle to the ground.

"Among the *Tosi Tivo,* all have spoken to the Comanches with a forked tongue. But my spirit tells me there is one who speaks true words. Come down from your horse and follow me."

Sam started to dismount, until the pain in his right foot reminded him that he could not walk behind Chama.

"I can't walk," Sam said, grinning. "My right leg is full of water. I am burdened with the old man's sickness in my bones. I'll have to ride wherever you want me to go."

Chama walked to the buckskin and took Sam's reins. Their eyes met briefly, Chama meeting Sam's clear blue eyes with a look of understanding.

"We have both seen many taums, Man-Who-Wears-The-Star. For us, so little time is left. Come, and I will show you why I have ridden so hard to stay ahead of the soldiers. When you see Pena Pah, you will understand why this place calls to my spirit across the miles, and your heart will know why I cannot go back with you to the reservation."

Chama led the horse down the passage, winding around tight turns where the walls were decorated with carved figures, pictures of horses and buffalo and deer, a story told in etched lines about the history of Chama's people.

At a sharp turn the passage ended. Chama led the gelding to a rise above a yawning valley more than a hundred feet below. Sam looked in silent awe at the tree-studded valley floor, following the course of a slender ribbon of water from one end to the other, sparkling in the sunlight. In the barren region surrounding Palo Duro, the canyon was an oasis, thick with deep green foliage along the winding course of the stream. Grass grew knee-high in the open meadows. He saw several ponies grazing contentedly below a sheer wall at one side of the canyon. The place Chama called Pena Pah was a dreamlike setting, a silent hollow in the limestone mountain.

Chama walked to a ledge above the trail leading into the valley, sweeping a hand across the canyon below.

"This is why I have come, *Tosi Tivo*. This is where my heart has been for eighteen taums."

The sun was a crimson ball on the horizon as Sam reined his buckskin into the basin. Tom had a fire going in a thicket of mesquites. The wind carried the scent of coffee across the basin as Sam trotted over to the fire and climbed down.

"Find anything?" Tom asked, slurping coffee while he spoke.

Sam did not reply immediately, not until he poured himself a cup of Tom's coffee and settled beside the fire.

"A dead end," he said finally, gazing at the sunset. "How about you? Find any tracks?"

"Just muddy ground," Tom replied, thinking there was something odd about Sam's voice. "I reckon the rain wiped out anything we might have found. Those Indians could have gone any direction. It'll take the whole United States Army to find them now. How's the ankle?"

For a moment Tom could not be sure Sam heard the question. His face was turned to the brilliant sunset, seemingly lost in thought.

"It hurts some," Sam said a moment later. "Ran out of whiskey. I don't suppose there's another bottle tucked away in your saddlebags."

"I wish there were. Right now, I'm ready for a stiff drink. Been a long four days. I guess we'll be heading home. No sense in lookin' for something that isn't there."

Sam nodded, still gazing at the distant sunset as if his thoughts were millions of miles away.

"I doubt if anybody will ever find 'em, Tom. This is a big place. The thing to remember is these men are Comanches. Since I first started trackin' Indians, none of the rest even came close to hidin' tracks like a Comanche. There've been times I came along, following a set of hoofprints, and then they just stopped. The only way a mounted Indian could have left the spot without leavin' some tracks would be if he sprouted wings, like Quinne."

"Like what?" Tom asked, puzzled by the unfamiliar word.

"Like an eagle," Sam said softly.

Two days later they met Capt. Lloyd Braverman's

column on the bank of the rain-swollen river. Their camp was in disarray, men sprawled under shade trees, exhausted and saddle-sore. Sam rode to the nearest campfire and climbed down, wincing as his ankle touched the ground.

Captain Braverman walked over, his face red from too much sun and drying wind. He shook hands with Sam and Tom, offering coffee while the two marshals found shade from an afternoon sun.

"How did you get in front of us?" Braverman asked. "We've been pushing so hard, we lost almost half our horses."

"We rode the train to Childress," Sam replied, leaning back against the trunk of a live oak.

"Did you find any sign of the Comanches?"

Sam shook his head, watching the worn troopers camped along the river.

"Big rain wiped out all their tracks. You might as well turn back, Cap'n. I'm headed for Childress to file my report, then we'll be on the next train for Lawton. A man could spend the rest of his life in those canyons and never sight them. It would take two or three thousand men to comb every one of those ravines leading from the river. My advice is you start back, as soon as your men are able to travel. You ain't got near enough men and horses to do the job without tracks to follow. Besides, I don't figure the army brass will want to waste very much more taxpayers' money lookin' for four Comanches."

Braverman turned abruptly and stared at Sam.

"Only four?" he asked, his voice betraying surprise. "We were told it was fifty or more. I saw all those tracks myself. How could it be just four?"

Sam shook his head, thinking of all the furor caused by Ike Tatum's story for the newspapers.

"Just ten ponies, Cap'n, and five Indians to start with. We found one of them in a shallow grave just before it rained. The other ponies were spare mounts, so they could outride your cavalry on fresher horses and build up a big lead. But right now, they're down to three ponies, and only four Indians. A military man ain't gonna make much of a name for himself if he spends two or three months tryin' to locate four Indians, 'specially with almost a hundred troopers. A thing like that, it could look like hell on a man's record, like he didn't know what he was about out in the field."

Braverman glanced at his men lounging around their campfires.

"You're probably right, Marshal. We started out with eighty mounted men, and as of this morning, only fifty-two still have serviceable horses. The rest went lame on this rough ground. I expected our horses . . . and the men, to be in better shape. We left the cripples at a ranch down the river. Almost half my men are down to boot leather."

Sam tossed down his coffee and lay back on the grass with his Stetson over his face, shielding his eyes from the glare.

"I'd turn back, if it was me, Cap'n," he said. "As the U.S. Marshal in charge of this manhunt, I'm calling it quits for my branch of the service. You can go on, if you've nothing better to do, but I'd hate like hell to have to answer to the brass if they ask why you spent all summer lookin' for four runaway Indians. Besides, a man's ass can get mighty sore, sittin' a saddle for a couple of months."

Braverman gazed thoughtfully at the river, working the muscles in his cheeks.

"It would seem we failed miserably," he said, color rising in his cheeks. "I pushed the men as hard as I could."

Sam lifted the brim of his hat, watching Braverman's youthful face with some amusement.

"You've got plenty of company, Cap'n, when it comes to chasin' Comanches. Plenty of men in uniform have tried catchin' up with them over the last fifty years. Ain't many can say they even came close."

Sam closed his eyes, resting in the shade while he thought about Braverman's frustration at being unable to find the escaped Indians. Even if Braverman went on to the canyon, he would never stand a chance of locating Chama. The boy was too young to know what tracking Comanches was all about, born too late to have seen firsthand how a mounted Comanche could just disappear into thin air.

12

Sam applied the brakes and felt the Star shudder as it came to a stop in front of the agency office. Steam hissed from the radiator cap as he reached for the walking stick and got down from the seat, slowly putting weight on his bandaged right foot before he started the walk toward the steps. Using the cane was a final blow to his pride, but at Dr. Robert's insistence he was wearing a bedroom slipper on the bad foot and walking with the cane. He thought himself to be a tragic sight, hobbling along on his cane, hoping no one was looking as he mounted the steps and reached for the door. He glanced toward the barracks and shacks of the reservation, thankful that the compound looked empty, until he noticed an Indian staring at him from the shade of a porch. There could be no doubt that the Indian was watching him, for he was alone in the agency parking lot, except for a scattering of chickens.

He stopped, for there was something familiar about the distant face. He knew he should recognize the woman, but for the moment he could not recall a name.

He opened the door and forgot about the woman, for this meeting with the Assistant Commissioner from the Bureau of Indian Affairs in Washington had kept him awake most of last night, tossing and turning, considering all the grim possibilities. When word came yesterday that the commissioner had arrived on the train from Washington to look into the Comanche affair, Sam knew the search for Chama could begin again on a grand scale. Like twenty years before, the army could send thousands of troops to Palo Duro with seasoned Indian trackers to flush Chama from his hiding place. If Ike Tatum created enough fuss, the higher-ups would have no choice. They would make an example of the runaways, to discourage any others from making a similar attempt. If an all-out manhunt was ordered, Chama's freedom would be short, and probably result in a bloody ending in the peaceful little canyon he called Pena Pah. Sam knew beyond any doubt that Chama would never surrender. He would die in a last bid for freedom, rather than face a return to Fort Sill.

Sam hobbled to the back office, feeling foolish wearing one slipper and one boot. The man from Washington would probably regard anything Sam said as the babblings of some old coot whose mind had begun to wander with advanced age. He was curious as to why he had been invited to this meeting at all, since it was an affair for the bureau and the army. Chama had committed no act of violence on his flight through Oklahoma and Texas, at least nothing severe enough to bring forth any warrants for his arrest from local peace officers. In the week following Sam's return to the fort, no word had come back of any criminal charges, although an uncounted number of wire fences had been cut. But it was not enough to warrant any legal action, for his office had not received a single request for Chama's arrest.

Sam opened the office door and went in. Walter Townsend sat across the desk beside a neatly dressed man of about fifty, a starched white collar and bow tie puckering the flesh of his neck.

Ike Tatum glanced up as Sam walked in. Tatum's face did not reflect the satisfaction Sam had expected from the visit by the bureau commissioner. Tatum's eyes held a wary look, as if an earlier discussion had not gone quite as he planned.

The commissioner stood up as Sam approached a chair, extending a handshake, all the while giving Sam a look of appraisal.

"I'm William Bibb with the Bureau of Indian Affairs in Washington. You must be Marshal Sam Ault."

Sam nodded, accepting the handshake, feeling a soft palm that was seldom employed in any physical labor.

"Pleased to meet you, Mr. Bibb," Sam said, looking at Walter Townsend as he sat in a vacant chair. Townsend's face also warned that this meeting had not gone well before Sam arrived. His face was tight across the bones of his skull, lips pressed firmly together.

"We've been talking about this matter concerning the Comanches," Bibb began, his voice crisp. "Since you followed their tracks to this canyon in Texas, I wanted your opinion on a few things."

Sam put his cane beside himself on the floor and waited. There was a keen edge in Bibb's voice, slicing through to the core of things.

"My deputy and I stayed on the tracks maybe six or

213

seven miles up the canyon. At dark we met a big rain-storm, three or four inches in a few hours. Washed out all the tracks. Nothing left for us to follow, so we turned back. That's the long and the short of it. A place that big, it could take weeks, maybe months, to pick up sign again, if you ever found any."

Bibb frowned and folded his hands.

"I checked your record when I arrived yesterday, Marshal. It appears you are regarded as the best tracker in this part of the country. You have a fine record. I think it is safe to assume that if *you* couldn't find any tracks, there weren't any. In your opinion, how many Comanches were out there?"

"Four," Sam replied, giving Tatum a quick look. "We found a grave in the canyon, an old Indian named Quahip. From the looks of the corpse, he'd been dead several days. Bullet hole in the neck. Before the rain came, I found the tracks of the other four. Best I could tell, the other four made it."

Bibb gave Tatum a sharp look.

"Four," Bibb said evenly. "We received initial reports that the group was much larger. However, in light of your experience tracking Indians, we can agree that there were four in this party."

Sam nodded, wondering about the looks Bibb was giving Tatum.

"It would appear, then," Bibb continued, "that the records kept on these people here at Fort Sill are inaccurate. Mr. Tatum tells me he is having trouble coming up with a complete list of the ones who are missing. Either there is another group of Indians out there someplace, or the records here are badly kept. I've been going through the files, and it seems Mr. Tatum can't account for all his Indians. Some, I discovered, have been dead for several years, but the files still list them as receiving a ration. While this doesn't concern you, Marshal Ault, I mention it only to point out why I needed to talk with you personally. You saw the tracks, and you tell me there were only four."

Sam felt the heat from Tatum's eyes before he answered.

"Just four. Three old men and a boy of fourteen. In my opinion, they're harmless. The old men just wanted to be free of the reservation for a while. They're in their sixties and seventies, the last of the old-time warriors who couldn't adjust to reservation life, after so long as free roaming Indians. They won't bother anybody, in my opinion, if they're left alone. Probably just hunt a few deer and live like they did before. At their age, there isn't much harm left in them."

Bibb nodded thoughtfully.

"But what about the boy? By law, he should be in school."

Sam thought about his answer before he spoke.

"Won't be long until the old men are dead, maybe a few years at the most, and then he'll be alone. I figure he'll come back, rather than live in that desolate place all by himself. There isn't a living soul in those parts for about a hundred miles in any direction. He'll come back when he gets tired of being lonely."

Bibb loosened his stiff collar with a finger and picked up a sheaf of papers.

"So far, there aren't any reports of violence perpetrated by those Comanches. We found a place in Texas where some of their horses were killed, but the Indians ran away without causing any casualties."

215

Sam glanced at Walter Townsend, watching the color rise in his cheeks.

"My office has not received any reports of trouble. A bunch of fences cut, but nothing serious."

Bibb nodded and stacked the papers neatly on Tatum's desk.

"It is your opinion, then, Marshal Ault, that these four will not act violently on citizens in the region around this Palo Duro canyon?"

Sam could not suppress a chuckle.

"At their age, Mr. Bibb, they're lucky to be able to walk. I doubt anybody will ever hear about them again. Bein' Comanches, they know how to hide their tracks from most anybody. Unless somebody goes lookin' for them, they won't leave those empty canyons. That's my guess."

Bibb seemed finished with the matter and stood up.

"Thank you for coming, Marshal Ault. I appreciate your honest answers. We'll handle the situation from here."

Sam found his cane and struggled to his feet.

"I don't suppose it matters," Sam said offhandedly, "but I'm curious. What do you intend to do about them?"

Bibb turned to Ike Tatum and leveled a hard look as he spoke.

"Officially, we'll continue looking for them when manpower permits, and list them as missing. Unofficially, Mr. Tatum will be pretty busy correcting some discrepancies in his records, and Major Townsend will have most of his available men employed in making some drastic changes in conditions around here. There is a growing list of things sorely in need of attention at

216

this reservation. Both these men will probably be too busy to do very much looking around for a while."

Sam shook hands with Bibb and limped toward the door. He did not need to look back to make certain that Tatum and Townsend were watching him, for he could feel their eyes on his back as he left the room.

Sam walked out in the blinding sunlight and started for his car, until he saw someone from the corner of his eye, standing in the shade of a porch at a shack near the edge of the Indians' quarters. He stopped, and looked again at the old woman who had watched him enter the office. She was standing in the same spot, piercing him with a look. He could not remember where he had seen her before, but there was something familiar about her and he knew he should remember her name.

He gave her a wave and turned for his car, until he heard a frail voice call out to him from the porch.

"Tosi Tivo . . . did the soldiers find my grandson?"

Sam stopped and faced the old woman. She was Pohawcut, the wife of Buffalo Hump. Without her black mourning paint, he had not recognized her.

"They are gone," Sam said in Comanche.

Pohawcut left her porch, taking tentative steps toward Sam, turning often to watch for anyone who might be listening. She came to him and stopped, her eyes filled with the agony of her loneliness, and whispered a question.

"Did they find the Palo Duro?"

Sam stared down on her deeply wrinkled face, thinking of what he might say that would comfort her.

"If I tell you true words, you must not repeat them, Pohawcut. The lives of Chama, and your grandson, will depend on your silence."

217

She gave the sign of agreement quickly, her eyes pleading.

"They are in Palo Duro, at the canyon called Pena Pah. They are safe from the soldiers. No one will ever find them."

Tears streamed down Pohawcut's face. Her hands shook as she wiped them away.

"What of Poke? Salope dreams of him in the dark, and prays for his safety."

"He is with the others. Only Quahip walks in the spirit world. You must not try to follow, for it will lead the soldiers to their hiding place. Their lives depend on your silence."

Pohawcut lowered her eyes and sobbed openly, keeping the sounds in her chest, overcome by a mixture of grief and happiness. Then she stopped and looked deeply into Sam's eyes, her lips trembling. She took a small leather pouch from her neck, dangling on a rawhide thong, and placed it in Sam's hands.

"It is the medicine bundle of Buffalo Hump, prepared for him by the great shaman *Isa Tai*. It will drive the evil spirits from your leg, Man-Who-Wears-The-Star. It is all I have to give for the words of truth you have spoken."

13

Tom Ford picked up the newspaper from the pile of mail and carried it into his study. He switched on a lamp and settled into his easy chair, scanning the headlines for the latest news about the war. Four days earlier, on December 7, the Japanese had hurled their bombs down on Pearl Harbor, pulling the United States into the Second World War. The front page of the *Oklahoma City Tribune* was filled with stories of war preparations, and the first pictures of the destruction at Pearl Harbor. Tom began reading on page 1, then he turned to the back of his paper for a continuation of the events that would bring the whole country into the fight.

He almost missed a short item on the back page, buried between a grocery advertisement and the obituaries. But his eyes strayed to a short clip from Amarillo, Texas, carried by a national wire service, that began with a bold caption: LONE COMANCHE INDIAN SURRENDERS IN TEXAS.

Tom sat up quickly and found his reading glasses, then he read carefully down the page.

A party of local ranchers and Amarillo peace officers have finally put an end to the stories circulating around the panhandle region that a tribe of wild Indians still lived in the Palo Duro Canyon. For many years ranch hands reported seeing a few horseback Indians in the area, but most scoffed at these stories as the product of too much boredom and bottled whiskey among cowboys.

Last week, the stories took on a new reality, as a group of mounted men followed horse tracks to a secluded spot in the northern reaches of Palo Duro Canyon, where they found a lone Indian who says he is the only survivor of a band of Comanche Indians who escaped from Fort Sill, Oklahoma, at the turn of the century. The captive Indian speaks some English, and identified himself as John Yellow Bull of the Kwahadie Comanche tribe. According to his story, he escaped from the reservation with a few older Comanches when he was a child, and has lived in the canyon since, existing on wild game and roots of exotic plants.

John Yellow Bull is reported to be in his fifties, and from the evidence around his campsite, he has lived in the area for some time in a shelter built from animal skins. Members of the search party took photographs of the Indian and his home, which are on display at the Amarillo

Public Library during December and January.

At this time the Indian is awaiting transfer to a reservation in Oklahoma. Hundreds of curious visitors have flocked to the city jail for a glimpse of Amarillo's savage Comanche, however officials at the jail state that their Indian is quite friendly, in spite of his savage appearance. When captured, he wore only animal skins and long braided hair, and carried a handmade bow and crude arrows. The capture brings to an end the folktales about wild Indians still living in the panhandle. The last wild Indian in Texas surrendered peacefully without a fight.

Tom put down the paper and removed his glasses, thinking back to the time he and Sam Ault rode the train to Childress, then horseback across the plains to the Palo Duro canyon, in search of escaping Comanches from Fort Sill. Tom was sure one of the Indians was named John Yellow Bull, the boy who rode with old Toyah Chama and the others. It was a long time ago, and his memory was admittedly a bit dim, but he was sure the name was the same. John Yellow Bull was the boy who rode with Chama.

He remembered Sam, dead since 1917, and recalled how close he had felt to the man who recommended him for the job at Cache as marshal. He remembered, too, how odd it seemed at the time, when he and Sam came back to Cache without staying on the trail of the Indians. Tom had always held a secret suspicion that Sam found the Comanches on the day they split up in the canyon. Sam seemed different after that particular

221

day, and two weeks after they got back to Cache, he took an early retirement. He blamed it on his ailing knees, but Tom suspected otherwise. Something happened up there in the canyon, something that made Sam quit his job two months early. And once they got back home, Sam never mentioned the Indians again, at least not to Tom. Odd, for a man who had been a friend of the leader of the runaways, the one called Chama.

Tom walked to a window and gazed at the busy streets of Cache, cars speeding past his house in both directions, as he thought about the story in the *Tribune* and the ride with Sam Ault to the Palo Duro. It had all been a long time ago. Now, as America entered its second big war, Tom was near retirement himself. The story of the lone Indian brought back a flood of old memories, days spent riding the high bluffs with the big man who had been his friend. It did not matter then, and certainly did not matter now, that Sam might have found the Comanches and decided to let them go free. But it probably made a difference to Sam, and it would explain why he took his retirement two months early. Sam was like that . . . right was right and wrong was wrong, with no middle ground. Remembering it, Sam had asked Tom to file the report with headquarters at Fort Smith. It was a technicality, not signing the false report, but probably something Sam's rigid set of rules required. It all fit, thinking back on it. Sam Ault never failed to follow an order, or do his duty if he could. It made sense now, after reading the story in the paper. Sam had found old Chama, but had no stomach for taking him back to the reservation. He simply rode away and said nothing, retiring early to silence his conscience.

Tom chuckled to himself. One thing was certain . . . Sam carried his secret with him to the grave. Now, over thirty years later, it really didn't matter to anyone, except to the man who called himself John Yellow Bull. And to the three old men who were allowed their last days on earth as free Comanches.

It was finished. *Suvate.*

THE SEVENTH CARRIER SERIES
By PETER ALBANO

THE SEVENTH CARRIER (2056, $3.95/$5.50)
The original novel of this exciting, best-selling series. Imprisoned in a cave of ice since 1941, the great carrier *Yonaga* finally breaks free in 1983, her maddened crew of samurai determined to carry out their orders to destroy Pearl Harbor.

THE SECOND VOYAGE OF THE SEVENTH CARRIER (2104, $3.95/$4.95)
The Red Chinese have launched a particle beam satellite system into space, knocking out every modern weapons system on earth. Not a jet or rocket can fly. Now the old carrier *Yonaga* is desperately needed because the Third World nations—with their armed forces made of old World War II ships and planes—have suddenly become superpowers. Terrorism runs rampant. Only the *Yonaga* can save America and the Free World.

RETURN OF THE SEVENTH CARRIER (2093, $3.95/$4.95)
With the war technology of the former superpowers still crippled by Red China's orbital defense system, a terrorist beast runs rampant across the planet. Outarmed and outnumbered, the target of crack saboteurs and fanatical assassins, only the *Yonaga* and its brave samurai crew stand between a Libyan madman and his fiendish goal of global domination.

QUEST OF THE SEVENTH CARRIER (2599, $3.95/$4.95)
Power bases have shifted drastically. Now a Libyan madman has the upper hand, planning to crush his western enemies with an army of millions of Arab fanatics. Only *Yonaga* and her indomitable samurai crew can save the besieged free world from the devastating iron fist of the terrorist maniac. Bravely, the behemoth leads a rag tag armada of rusty World War II warships against impossible odds on a fiery sea of blood and death!

ATTACK OF THE SEVENTH CARRIER (2842, $3.95/$4.95)
The Libyan madman has seized bases in the Marianas and Western Caroline Islands. The free world seems doomed. Desperately, *Yonaga's* air groups fight bloody air battles over Saipan and Tinian. An old World War II submarine, *USS Blackfin*, is added to *Yonaga's* ancient fleet and the enemy's impregnable bases are attacked with suicidal fury.

TRIAL OF THE SEVENTH CARRIER (3213, $3.95/$4.95)
The enemies of freedom are on the verge of dominating the world with oil blackmail and the threat of poison gas attack. *Yonaga's* officers lay desperate plans to strike back. Leading a ragtag fleet of revamped destroyers and a single antique World War II submarine, the great carrier must charge into a sea of blood and death in what becomes the greatest trial of the Seventh Carrier.